MW01165674

The
DESTRUCTION
of a
Psychopath
by an
AMERICAN
Beauty

SAM DRAUT

authorHOUSE®

AuthorHouse™
1663 Liberty Drive
Bloomington, IN 47403
www.authorhouse.com
Phone: 1 (800) 839-8640

Published by AuthorHouse   04/30/2020

ISBN: 978-1-7283-2433-3 (sc)
ISBN: 978-1-7283-2432-6 (e)

Library of Congress Control Number: 2019912422

Print information available on the last page.

To Jessica for demanding more and more from me
when I first started writing it,
To David for helping me analyze the direction of it,
To Charlotte for showing me what it was all about.

1

He had nothing to say.

He couldn't produce any empathy as the girl he had known for several months spoke about her father with throat cancer. It wasn't lack of compassion that disconnected Jason Vaughn from Ashley and her father's diagnosis. He worked with her for the summer and shared a brief moment of intimacy with her, but none of the previous moments emotionally attached him to her.

Jason remembered waving to her lonely father as Ashley walked toward his car on their only date months earlier. He didn't place any value on the brief encounter with a man dying due to having smoked too many cigarettes.

Before Ashley noticed his disengagement, Jason forced himself to ask questions to mask his indifference. He tried to sincerely show concern as the lights reflected off the computer screens in the office.

She answered his questions without any doubt of his interest. Ashley shared intimate details while Jason listened. He smiled and nodded, changing facial expressions and presenting the appearance of an intentional listener.

Jason was fond of Ashley.

She was young and vibrant with bleached blond hair and a brimming smile of hope. He was attracted to her personality because she was confident and educated, but he couldn't force himself to feel anything for her.

Ashley was what Jason wanted in a girl, and plenty like her were attracted to him, but now, Ashley's father had cancer.

While Ashley continued to talk, Jason thought of his first meeting with her and how it was the best moment they shared. His initial encounter with anyone was always the best moment for Jason. The uncertainty of what would come next was intriguing to him. Once the beginning had passed, there was no nervous energy and forced small talk became common interactions.

So instead of typing final edits for the Louisville Business Weekly publication for the next morning, Jason pretended to console Ashley about her dying father. In Jason's mind, it wasn't Ashley's problem, it was her father's issue. He was the one with cancer. He was the one forced to deal with the consequences of smoking for 40 years.

By Jason's logic, there was no reason Ashley should be upset by any of it, and certainly no reason for him to sit through 15 minutes of bereavement.

Jason didn't know the man and never would. Ashley was a merely a fading moment in Jason's life, so her current problem seemed irrelevant to him, he thought.

As he listened to her talk, he looked at her green eyes. He could see her affection for her father. The night they shared together meant more to her, which explained her comfort in sharing details with him, though it had meant nothing to Jason.

Jason was flattered by Ashley's attachment to him; after all, Jason never questioned his own physical appeal. Like others he knew, he considered himself more than worthy of garnering attention and affection. He always had.

His boyish smile and youthful arrogance were considered charming by many. He seemed younger than his mid-twenties and had yet to see himself as a mature adult.

He didn't find Ashley boring, but one night together had been enough. Their past was untouchable and forever unchangeable, a notion of brevity that was enough for Jason. So, he was left listening to her talk about her dying father.

I like to talk to myself. Sometimes I think people notice. I don't really care though, they probably just think that I'm crazy, which is okay, because I already know I am. I'm good at pretending a lot of things, but being sane isn't one.

The night wouldn't end until 10 p.m., when final pages were submitted for printing, so while pretending to be actively listening to Ashley, Jason would occasionally glance at the time at the bottom right hand corner of his computer screen.

It was 9:27 p.m.

She can't talk for another 33 minutes. I don't even have enough work for another 33 minutes. Isn't it funny, people don't really listen, they're just waiting for their moment to talk? Maybe I should buy her a voice recorder, it would be doing the same thing that I'm doing right now.

"But what about you?" Ashley asked.

The obligatory question directed at me. That's the first one tonight. After talking for so long, people get the urge that it's mandatory to ask the listener a question, like it quells any notion of the conversation being one-sided. I prefer to stay one-sided; it really makes for awkward conversations when those questions are forced.

"Have you seen Brad lately?" Jason responded. He tended to counter with more questions to avoid revealing any details of his personal life.

Jason had worked at the Business Weekly as a copy editor for the print edition for two years. It only required a few hours a week that added supplemental income to his regular job. He attended weekly meetings on Friday mornings and edited pages Thursday nights, fixing infrequent errors left by the writers.

Ad placement was completed Thursday nights before submission to the printing press, so Ashley, the company's advertising director, was always present when Jason edited pages.

Typically, there were other writers in the small office typing out final additions to their stories or searching for the next idea. This night, however, Jason and Ashley were the only two left.

If Brad was here, I wouldn't have to listen to any of this. I haven't seen him in weeks. I'd rather hear about him than her dying father.

Jason was struck with relief when Ashley announced all the advertisements had been placed. He converted the pages to PDFs and sent the files to the printing press. Now, he could leave.

"All right, well everything's good to go, can I walk you to your car?"

Please say no.

Ashley accepted his offer, smiling at his chivalry. Part of Jason's charm was how polite he always was to others, which was only one reason why so many people thought so highly of him.

Jason found it humorous thinking people he spent just a few hours a week with had built such a façade of him in their minds. His coworkers at the Business Weekly thought highly of him, even though he merely showed up twice a week to fix their minor mistakes.

The night was still warm even though the summer sun had set an hour ago. The two reached their lone cars in the parking lot across the street as city lights filled the night sky.

"Even with my dad and work, I still have some free time every once in a while," Ashley said.

I like directness. I don't understand why people passively fidget around what they want.

"We can get together some time if you want. You need a little fun with everything you're going through," Jason said.

He had no intention of seeing Ashley outside of the Business Weekly's office, but trusted his ability to continue to defer another date with her.

Jason thought highly of Ashley. She was young and attractive, just like him. Their personalities paired well together, but there was something missing in her. She could make his nerves pick up for a second, but for just a second, and he wanted there to be more.

He settled into his car, taking one final look at her short hair, lightly freckled face still teeming with youth and wonder, before she drove off into the city streets.

It's better to leave things this way.

Jason rolled down his windows and played modern classical music that helped him slow his mind into a quiet night as he drove back to his apartment. He didn't want to feel sad nor would he, but the gentle piano music was a gateway to lead him to deeper thought.

How am I going to continue to push Ashley aside? Why can't I feel the same way she feels about me?

One thought that didn't run through his mind: Ashley's father had cancer.

2

*J*ason could be put in a room filled with his closest friends and feel just as lonely as he would if he were sitting in his one-bedroom apartment by himself. He reiterated a favorite Joseph Conrad's phrase, "We live as we dream, alone."

Jason could move through a crowd of anonymous people and feed off of their energy, but in a crowd of people that knew him, he resorted to an ill-fated character, awaiting scripted responses.

Another night with these people and their sedated minds. People don't want to know the truth. They want to live in their protective bubble and not have to think about reality.

After walking up to the modest-sized house in St. Matthews, Jason paused just before the door, taking one more deep breath before exposing himself to hours of social interaction. He liked to watch his friends' interactions without intermingling himself. He wasn't sure if they altered their behavior when he was around, but he sometimes envisioned what their lives would be like if he was no longer a part of it.

Kyle and Julie sat together; the latter spread a worn smile on a simple face. Julie lived a fast life in her adolescence, so the somberness of middle age appealed to her more than her others.

No one questioned Julie's energy and youth because of her lively demeanor, no one except Jason. He knew she was closer to an adult and parent than she was an unrelenting young woman, uninhibited by the responsibilities of age.

While Julie had some greater depth in her longing to remove herself from youth that Jason appreciated, Kyle fit an archetype that bored Jason. Kyle had been athletic and popular in his youth, went to college and left some of his best qualities behind as he developed.

Jason had been long-time friends with Kyle, but his fuller face and growing midsection had left Jason disgusted in recent years. His unkempt black hair aided the notion that everything good in his life had happened before the graduation of high school, and anything after that attributed to a slow decline. Jason had sympathy for Kyle, enough to override his disdain, and because of his long-term relationship with Julie, Jason accepted that Kyle was tolerable.

Julie and Kyle made each other happy, which was enough to allow Jason to pass along his blessing year after year. The two had been together long enough that finding another person would be a great inconvenience for either, so a fate intertwining them together had already been affirmed. Though neither of the two realized it yet, Jason did.

Jason was in a good mood, so the small gathering of close friends would be nice. He had not watched anything recently on television that caught his eye, so he had no character to portray this night.

There were times when Jason could watch or read about a fictional character and become them for a day. Their quotes and mannerisms filled his mind, allowing him to become the character as if he had rehearsed a script.

Some people picked up on his character transformations while other observers remained oblivious.

He opened the door and his presence was announced by cheers of his six closest friends. Once again, he was the center of attention, just the way he needed it to be.

Kyle stood up and shook Jason's hand while all eyes landed on him.

"I'm the only reason you guys stay together," Jason said.

Everyone laughed, but Jason knew this was the furthest thing from the truth. He feared they knew that as well.

Jason became a part of the friend group years earlier when Julie invited him to a party she was hosting. He had known Kyle as well, and though the combination of those two disinterested Jason within days, their group of friends intrigued him enough to stick around.

Julie realized she couldn't understand Jason's eccentricity, so she passed him along to her other friends in hopes that somebody else would understand him.

Wherever he went, Jason left people captivated and confused as if they wanted a little more information about who he was. Jason deflected questions and hid enough about himself for people to wonder if there was more to him.

Of the six people encircling him, no one had yet dared to break open the enigma of Jason Vaughn. It's why Jason liked them so much, everyone except Naomi.

Naomi was unafraid and never hesitant around him. She asked questions that made him uncomfortable. He couldn't deflect her questions because they weren't asked as obligatory responses. She didn't wait for her turn to talk, she demanded answers.

He hated her.

But she challenged his intellect more than anyone else.

Jason hadn't found anyone who could see any depth in himself, so often the 30 seconds of conversation between him and Naomi completed his night. He enjoyed nights with his friends, but Naomi's questions and commentary pulled a string no one else seemed to notice.

He hated her, but he had an addiction to the nervous moments when she would escape her boyfriend Brandon to ask Jason one thing that could tear him apart for the night. Their conversations would haunt him for hours. He would drive back to his apartment with piano music playing, contemplating every word.

This night, Naomi's long, slender figure controlled the corner of the room. She was the first person Jason saw when he walked into the room of people. Naomi had a touch of elegance that escaped most people's attention, but she carried herself with subtle confidence of her own self-awareness.

If he wasn't blinded by his hatred for her, Jason would admit Naomi was appealing, in her own understated way. Her brown hair hung below her shoulders and it was rarely fixed perfectly. Her green eyes were deep and big, but she didn't wear enough makeup to draw attention to them, nor too little to turn attention away.

Brandon was nearby, but not close enough to share the corner with Naomi. Though the two had been together for more than a year, Naomi and Brandon were never considered a true couple by Jason. He knew that Naomi kept Brandon far enough away for her own independence, but close enough to keep him satisfied with their public interactions.

It's what Jason had come to realize about Brandon: he wanted to be a part of something. He was nice, relatively quiet and would only speak when spoken to in social settings. Brandon was always friendly to Jason and whoever else was around. Jason thought of Brandon as a casual, clueless observer of the group.

While Naomi drilled Jason with cringing questions about his life, Brandon never threatened Jason, which is why he developed a palatable taste for Brandon. Jason could hide however much he wanted from Brandon without much recourse.

One thing Jason appreciated about his group of friends was that there was nothing tying him to them.

He had spent a night with Heather, but there was no sexual interest drawing him into the crowd, or a dear enough friendship that he needed.

Brandon and Naomi had been together for more than a year and Julie and Kyle were nearing an engagement, meaning

11

Jason and Keshawn were free to roam without the group when they wished. Most people believed Jason and Keshawn were best friends, the latter would agree too, but Jason hesitated in admitting anything that made him seem human.

In actuality, though, the two were best friends by every other definition. Keshawn and Jason had known each other before Julie introduced Jason to her circle of friends, but their relationship grew as the social circle came together.

Keshawn was more social of the two and often convinced Jason to attend more events than he naturally would. Everyone liked Keshawn. He was handsome and friendly with positive energy that exuded confidence.

Someone is going to give in.

"Let's go to Circle's."

Of course, Heather had to suggest it. And once it gets suggested, it spreads like wildfire.

"All right, we haven't been in weeks, who's driving?"

Leave it to Kyle to take over the mission of getting to a local bar that's five minutes away.

"I'll get Ben to."

Right on queue Julie volunteers her 18-year-old brother to be the designated driver. I need to get away from these people. I can predict their every word. Here it comes; Brandon looks brave enough to make a joke about getting Ben into the bar.

"We can sneak Ben in for the night."

The other six began to talk back and forth while Jason slowly tuned them out.

I should have worn a better shirt.

"Let's go Jay."

He always enjoyed riding with his friends. On the drives, they would discuss music or what would happen next, and Jason felt a feeling of comfort knowing everyone was headed in the same direction, the youthful lives intermingling toward an undeniable, unalterable destination. The inevitable steps of aging moved closer and closer, but when everyone came together, the inescapable truth could be forgotten for a moment.

Jason knew he was getting older, he could feel it. Not in his body, but his mind. He dreaded getting older and if he could just hold off aging, he could stave off the mounting responsibilities of middle age.

Circle's was packed with people, but crowds didn't bother Jason as much as his other friends. He liked the energy and mingled with everyone. He never considered himself social, but he understood what people wanted to be asked and what they wanted to hear, so people enjoyed his presence.

See, when you're meeting a new person, there is no past and no foreseeable ending, so our energy can be dedicated to the potential of the unknown future.

Jason didn't have a problem getting free drinks at Circle's or any other bar. People were drawn to his attractiveness and once he caught their attention, there was nothing more he had to do.

His eyes were comforting to look at, but it was the enigma of Jason's personality that often drew strangers to him. His outward expressions portrayed his internal confidence while also succeeding to flash a brief inkling of something more being hidden.

Jason and Keshawn made their customary walk around the bar and its stained wooden floors, visiting with old and new friends alike in the dimmed lighting.

Jason liked going to bars with Keshawn. He liked being around Keshawn's energy - it gave him a glimpse into the social dynamic of being a black man in America. Jason had stood next to Keshawn when he had been denied entry to places because of his shoes, pants, hoodie and other things. It never seemed to bother Keshawn, but the denials infuriated Jason on behalf of his friend.

There's no point in small talk with people I used to know. Knowing what their current job is or relationship troubles doesn't affect me and I won't remember it. Why do we wander around tempting these people to talk to us? These people waste my time. 12:47, plenty of time left.

As much as Jason wanted to brush every irrelevant person away, his desire to please others won over, forcing him to play the role of an interested cohort. He took comfort in his ability to string along conversations without a hint of his internal disinterest.

Just like he did with Ashley earlier that week, he would listen, nod, smile and even ask a few questions to solidify his artificial interest.

Three questions…the first one is broad, the second one alters the subject and the third one builds on the answer of the second question. Enough to make people believe I care while being brief enough for me to leave the person satisfied. People will tell anyone almost anything if they think you're willing to listen.

I like the human nature of social outings. Hundreds of young people gather in a small building late at night and for what? What are we looking for? What brings us out to Circle's every Friday night?

If Jason had an observational strength while in a crowd, it was his ability to scan scores of people and pick out every face in it. As he gazed over the room, Julie waved him down from across the bar.

"Jason, Jason!"

Four drinks in and Julie is already gone.

Some people have no awareness, others have no self-awareness. Maybe it's a good thing. I have awareness of the world around me because there is no world within me to consume my thoughts. Some. people obsess over themselves, yet the world outside of me takes up most of my contemplations.

"You need to meet Megan. She writes for the Daily Chronicle and she needs a date for her awards banquet tomorrow night. I told her you'd go with her."

Great, a Saturday night to myself turned into a debutante ball because Julie can't handle alcohol.

Jason didn't like saying no, so he felt obligated to go with Julie's friend. To him, the word "no" was vile and absolute. It was uncompromising and unable to be manipulated or crafted.

"Oh, is she here?" Jason asked.

"She left a while ago, but you're picking her up at 6 tomorrow night."

Jason laughed and caught back up with Keshawn as the two continued to make their rounds.

Ben never attempted to sneak inside, so around 3 a.m., the group finally piled into an Uber to head back to Julie's house.

As they arrived at their original location, the crowded dispersed to their cars. As Julie was stumbling back to her house, she turned to Jason.

"Hey Jay, relax about tomorrow. Megan is a doll. It'll be fun, just be yourself."

Jason turned back around and continued to walk to his car; Naomi glanced over at him as Brandon started his black BMW to drive the two of them home.

"But if you had any idea how to be yourself, no one would find you interesting," Naomi said over her shoulder.

Before Jason could respond, Naomi opened passenger door of Brandon's car.

Jason smiled and waved goodbye. Once in his car, he turned on Ludovico Einaudi and drove back to his apartment, contemplating one thing:

Who actually is Jason Vaughn?

3

The setting summer sun shined off the yellow-painted brick house as Jason walked toward the door. The grass had turned dull brown after months in the scorching sun while the once manicured flowerbeds featured a lone white tulip oddly unusual for this late in the summer.

Without considering if it was polite or not, Jason reached to the bed to pull the weeds that stretched toward the single flower in the disheveled bed, but Megan stepped out of her front door just as he paused in front of the flower.

"You're even more handsome than Julie said."

That never gets old. Yet. I wonder how long it will last. People decline in beauty at different ages, some in their 30s, some in their 40s. How long would it be until I stopped getting that pleasantly surprised reaction from beautiful women on blind dates?

"I'm Megan Fairfield. I write for the Daily Chronicle, you work for the Business Weekly, right?"

"I do some stuff for them when I can, yeah," he said. "Jason Vaughn."

And that's all it takes. Introductions are meaningless. We could walk around with name tags to prevent it. That's probably a privacy concern though. I don't like hellos or goodbyes, but introductions are even worse. Usually if the girl isn't attractive enough or the guy doesn't seem significant, I don't even remember their names. I'll recall faces, but if they can't offer something to me, there's no reason to waste space in my memory storing their names and complicated histories.

I'll remember Megan's name because it's more than a 30-second encounter, and she's Julie's friend, but that might be the only thing that keeps her in my memory bank. Megan seems to be attractive and nice, but she's a walking cliché of social media obsessed, self-absorption that comes from trying too hard to fit into modern America's standard.

I heard once we can analyze people within two seconds of meeting them. Disinterested within two seconds seems too harsh, judgment within two minutes even sounds brutal, but three hours at an awards reception dinner might drive me insane. I wonder how many times she'll add it to her Snapchat story tonight. I don't even want to keep track.

To avoid $15 valet parking at the Galt House, the two parked a block and a half away and walked through the downtown streets in the fading sunlight. For the first time, Jason looked at her completely.

The black dress formed to Megan's figure while her heels made her legs look longer than they actually were. Her blond hair had dulled since its last bleach, but Jason could tell she hadn't let youth escape her yet.

As they walked toward the Galt House, Jason worried who might see them together. He thought of ways he could explain why they were together. Once the two reached the Ballroom on the second floor of the hotel, Jason knew the person he needed to be for the night.

Megan led him to the table occupied by her coworkers. He smiled and shook everyone's hands as he joked with the people around him.

"How did Megan convince you to come with her tonight?"

"Convince? She's paying me by the hour," Jason said, resulting in more than modest laughter. Megan and her coworkers continued to intermingle, but once a lull in the conversation started, they turned their gazes to Jason expectantly.

He shared several stories and jokes he had memorized, captivating the attention of the entire table. As he recited his rehearsed lines, their eyes lit up, and when he delivered punch lines, Megan's coworkers erupted in laughter. Cleverly, Jason stuttered and paused several times to make them believe all his material was all coming straight from his head.

"I think they like you more than me," Megan whispered to Jason after one of his stories.

I can't carry the bulk of this conversation much longer. I'm going have a smile frozen to my face.

"Do you want to grab us some drinks?" Megan asked.

"There's an open bar back there," one of Megan's coworkers pointed.

I can take a break for a few minutes.

Jason finished a drink at the bar and brought back another two drinks. Following his return, he could sense expectations rising as everyone's eyes landed back in his direction.

"Do you guys have a microphone I could use?" Jason joked, and once again, began his routine.

He planned another trip to the bar to break from the table's spotlight, but his intention was foiled when one of Megan's coworkers brought back a drink for him. The entrée portion of the meal was brought out to tables just as Jason began to feel himself wearing thin from the continuous social stimulation.

He finished the food faster than anyone else. He couldn't taste much of it considering he was so focused on smiling and keeping the conversation going.

I'll go to the bathroom and the bar; that will burn off 10 minutes.

Jason excused himself to the restroom as his audience urged him to come back quickly.

As he walked back from the restroom, Jason needed his reprieve to last longer. He went to get another drink, resting his forearms on the bar.

"You're doing a good job pretending like you belong here."

Jason paused, turning to see a young man in a red tie and navy suit next to him at the bar.

"How do you know I'm not a journalist?" Jason asked.

"Your suit is way too expensive for a journalist."

The two laughed as the bartender handed them drinks.

"Girlfriend or wife?"

"First date," Jason admitted.

"Bumble or Tinder?"

"Friend of a friend, actually," Jason answered.

"Which table?"

Jason pointed toward Megan, who was conversing with her coworkers.

"Oh, the Daily Chronicle, I bet you're the center of attention with that group," the young man in the navy suit and red tie said.

"I know, it's like I'm their entertainment for the evening," Jason said.

They both leaned back onto the bar and looked around the crowded ballroom.

"They did a psychological study," the young man in the navy suit and red tie started, "ranking people's positive energy on a scale of 1 to 10. Then they put all the people that scored a five in one room and added one person that scored a 10 in with them. The people did group work, activities and ate together. When they left, all those people that had scored a five suddenly were scoring six or seven. The positive energy of one person is infectious, it lifts up the morale of everyone else."

"You think I'm the 10 at a table of 5s?" Jason asked.

"I'm saying the study never considered fluctuations in positive energy. It's easy to be a different character for just one night," the young man in the navy suit and red tie took a sip from his cup. "Well, better get back to my table."

Curious, Jason lightly reached out his hand, "Your name?"

"We can skip introductions, neither of us will remember names," the young man in the navy suit and red tie answered.

"Usually I'd agree with you, but you have my curiosity and attention," Jason said.

"I'm Sam Draut, I work for a newspaper you'll never read." He walked into the crowd of people.

Jason turned back to the bartender and asked for another drink, prepared to return to the table with Megan's demanding coworkers.

The lights began to flicker signifying the beginning of the awards presentation.

Though exhausted, he would admit the first hour and a half had been fun and sitting through the final portion of the reception dinner without the spotlight was a drag. All the attention he held vanished with the dimming lights.

From a proud thespian to a silent onlooker, I'm a little more upset than I thought I would be.

The awards presentation continued as Jason finished his sixth drink.

I could walk out right now. I'd probably never hear from her again. I could start driving and just not stop until I found a place I liked.

He looked at Megan, who smiled at him and then returned her attention to the awards presentation. They had been together for several hours now, but Jason had yet to actually think about her.

He noticed an immaturity in her face, as if she had passed adolescence, but skipped the first half of her 20s, somehow awakening on the wrong side of 25. Her green eyes and face were simple, if not underwhelming. She was the epitome of a middle-class, Midwestern American, nothing more and nothing less.

The presentation ended, and lights returned, indicating the revival of comedian and entertainer Jason Vaughn. The table members said goodbye to Jason as they filtered out of the room, but he didn't remember any of their names. It wasn't that he didn't want to take the time to remember their names, but as he and Megan left the Galt House, he realized none of them struck him as significant.

There isn't anything better than walking and admiring the city lights at night with a beautiful girl. Megan isn't beautiful, but she's attractive, attractive enough for me to not be embarrassed walking a few blocks with her.

When they returned to the car, Megan showered Jason with compliments for the part he played in her "wonderful evening." She spoke with excitement while he calmly listened showing a fake smile. Once again, Jason had nothing to say.

At the yellow brick house, Megan asked the question Jason knew was coming since the moment he opened his car door hours earlier.

"Want to come inside?"

Jason saw no reason to say no, so he nodded and parked the car a few hundred feet down the street.

Instead of walking into a quiet household and going straight to Megan's bedroom, which Jason expected, several people were crowded in the living room as they walked through the door.

Jason scanned the room as Megan began to introduce him to some of her friends.

It was late, and he was bored, so his valiant effort at the

awards reception dinner would not transfer to the house. He had already used his character for the night, so he didn't feel an urge to use another fake persona.

Unstartling and apathetic, Jason intermingled with the other house guests. He could sense people in the room thought him as boring and disinteresting, just as he had viewed the crowd surrounding him hours earlier.

He became so removed from the conversation that he decided to walk into the kitchen for water and debated slipping out of the back door.

He filled a glass and turned around to rest his elbows on the countertop. He could feel the alcohol as fatigue filled his neck and shoulders. His hand became cold from holding the glass of water.

The kitchen was relatively clean, the refrigerator had a dry-erase board with a chore list and photos of who lived in the house. A lone banana rested in a basket next to several bottles of alcohol.

A young woman walked into the kitchen from the back hallway and stood a few feet away with a piercing stare directed at Jason. And then his heart jolted. He felt queasy and nervous – a new feeling to him. He stood frozen.

"I needed some water," she said.

She was beautiful, but Jason had seen beautiful before. She had something else, something more.

He thought her immaculate as her long hair reflected light from the lamp behind her. He was entranced by an utter flawlessness that surrounded her, as if after seeing her would ruin the rest of his life because no one would ever compare.

As quickly as she had appeared and interrupted Jason's inner thoughts, she disappeared into the dark hallway.

He felt shattered: someone so loudly burst into his life and promptly slipped away so quietly, someone who looked straight through him.

Though she exchanged a short greeting with him, Jason knew that she didn't know he existed, that he was insignificant to her, and because of this, his shoulders sunk in despair.

He turned and walked back into the crowded living room, incoherent voices of other guests filling his head.

4

Jason woke up the next morning with Megan beside him, her smeared makeup staining the crème colored pillowcases.

She looks awful.

He slipped out from underneath the sheets and put his clothes on. Startled by his rustling, Megan looked up and asked him to stay.

Jason glanced toward the window and saw the sun was high enough for him to begin the day. Megan rose as well and followed him.

He walked down the stairs of the second floor and looked toward the hallway in hopes that the girl from last night would once again appear. She didn't.

He didn't see her in the kitchen either, so he thought of her as an illusion, a beautiful apparition, never to be seen again.

The late morning sun was already beating on the yellow bricks as Megan opened the front door.

"Thank you for going with me last night, it couldn't have gone any better. I was so nervous about meeting you," Megan said.

Jason smiled and watched Megan's eyes build courage to speak again.

"Would you want to get together again sometime?" Megan asked.

At least she's being direct.

"Of course, I'll text you later tonight."

Jason walked toward his car, but before he opened his door, he turned to look back. He promised himself it wouldn't be the last time he would walk away from the brick house. His guarantee wasn't centered on Megan, instead, it was his desire to once again encounter the woman who saw through him.

He started his car and drove toward the rising sun.

Jason was meticulous about his physical appearance. Before he thought of fashion and style, he tailored his body. Few people could make him jealous, but he often wished upon his body similar sculpting from statues he saw in art museums.

With food and alcohol in his system from the prior night, he went to Seneca Park in hopes of running off excess weight.

Jason considered his mind scattered unless it was purposefully focused, which was something running did for him, allowing him to concentrate on his soft breath and light pounding of each step. His mind was most focused when he ran.

I can run in a park full of people and the only thing I aware of comprehend is myself. When I run, the outside world fades away and my own awareness is pointed inward.

After completing his run, Jason cooled down, walking

past children playing in the park. He wondered which ones would be like him.

"Where have you been?"

Jason turned to see Julie approaching, followed by Kyle and Naomi.

"We texted you about coming here today. How did last night go?"

"Sorry, my phone died."

"It must have gone well then," Julie answered snidely.

He knew an interrogation was coming from Julie. Kyle might even add in a few questions, but Jason was an expert at deflecting inquiries about his personal life.

"Did you spend the night?" Julie asked.

I don't get why people make sex out to be so taboo. It shouldn't be. If it was normal to everyone, we wouldn't have to go around bragging or complaining about it. Just think if sex was as normal as grocery shopping. It wouldn't be a conversation topic. How many times have you talked to someone about your trip to the grocery? Even if the produce is fresh and the self-checkout line is empty, you don't go around telling everyone about it.

"Yes," Jason said, shifting the conversation around the award reception.

"That sounds amazing, you have to see her again," Julie said, satisfied by Jason's description of the night.

The four walked to the tennis courts. Jason sat next to Naomi as they watched Kyle and Julie volley the ball back and forth.

Jason shook his head, "I may be taller, more attractive and a better athlete, but Kyle can definitely beat me in tennis."

Naomi laughed as Jason begrudgingly admitted defeat in one sport.

"Yeah, we all know you don't like to lose," Naomi said.

"That's why I won't play him."

"You only play if you know you're going to win."

Jason agreed with Naomi. He never wanted to be considered a loser.

In middle school, he studied and developed mannerisms to mimic the school's most popular boys. With his athletic abilities helping him develop friendships with teammates, he became popular in a few months.

No one knew where he came from or who he was, but they admired everything he did.

He pretended to be a popular adolescent and it worked. While other new students walked the hallways alone, Jason gained the attention and status he craved by becoming someone else entirely.

When the final bell rang, Jason was free from the charade, so his pretending rarely extended beyond school grounds. When other students invited him to social events outside of school, he declined. His character at school was enough to keep him popular, but too demanding to retain on a consistent basis.

Over time, the character he adapted continued to develop. He elevated his social status in high school. But as he grew older, it became necessary to end his time as a weekend recluse, so he did. When it was necessary for him to have a girlfriend, he found one. Whenever he needed to conform to the demand of the public, he did. And so, he became popular.

It was then that he began his caricatures, shifting from stars in movies, television shows or novels. With an ability to evolve and conform to multiple personalities, he could fit into any social group.

He became a self-proclaimed "man of the people." Yet as he always said, he had plenty of "penny friends" though no one knew him well.

Jason's closer friends and girlfriends struggled to decipher his life. As he grew closer to friends, teammates and peers, Jason feared being genuine would forfeit his status and people might not accept his true self.

"I've always gotten what I wanted," Jason muttered to Naomi. "I become so fixated on it, don't stop until I have it. If I dream it, I want it, if I want it, I get it."

Naomi nodded her head. "Do you have everything you want?"

"I think so."

"You may think you do, but you're always going to want more."

"Is that ever going to stop?" Jason asked.

"No. You're not the person you want to be, and you don't know how to be that person either."

Before Jason had time to respond, Julie rushed over to persuade the two to join her at Kyle's pool.

"Heather and Brandon are meeting us over there in 30 minutes."

"I have to take care of a few things, maybe another time," Jason said, heading away from the group.

Before reaching his car, Jason looked back at Naomi. The two locked eyes for a moment, then went their separate ways.

5

*J*eff Douglas is 38 years old and works at General Electric as a contract sales manager where he is paid $75,000 annually. He lives at 4327 Briarwood Avenue, Louisville Kentucky, 40207. He drives a silver Honda Civic and has been married for six years to a woman named Amy.

They have two children: Travis, 4, and Haley, 2. Jeff attended the University of Louisville and received a bachelor's degree in business administration. Jeff's favorite food is barbeque ribs, which he often makes himself, and he enjoys local craft beers.

He has trained for two mini-marathons, but has only run in one. Both of his parents are still living in the same house he grew up in. Jeff is a fan of the Cincinnati Bengals and supports his alma mater in collegiate athletics.

Jeff has been in love twice and has had his heart broken once. He is currently having an affair with Georgia Brooks, a 23-year-old coworker. It has been going on for the past seven months.

I know all of this because I have access to the internet.

And I won't forget any of this until the day I die.

People should be careful about what they put on social media. It makes their lives so public. What's even funnier is they don't realize how much information they put out there.

It can be fun to dig through a person's life with a search engine, but tonight I had a mission, and I got a little sidetracked. Douglas left his wallet in the booth of O'Charley's and I happened to be the next patron to sit in the booth.

Now, taking initiative regarding other people's affairs doesn't interest me usually, but for some reason, finding Jeff's wallet sparked something for me. I didn't have much to do tonight. It has been awhile since I broke down someone's life through observation and deduction.

Some people have secrets they like to keep, but one way or another, I eventually find out.

I took a psychology course in college and scored highest on facial recognition and awareness. I can see a person's facial expression for milliseconds and decide their emotion. A psychologist who had worked for 30 years couldn't comprehend and analyze as accurately as I could.

Okay, that's a bit of a stretch, but I had a natural ability that set me apart.

It's nice that I remember everything.

If I see a face once, I remember.

If I don't tell the person that I have seen them before, I don't think it's weird. I can't tell a girl that comes up to me at a bar that I saw her last week at Walgreen's. It wouldn't be right if I told her that I already know her name because I saw it on the computer screen on the cash register or that I scrolled through her Instagram and Facebook profile.

Do you ever feel like the person across from you is always a step ahead?

That's me, but I am three steps ahead and further along than you'll ever be. Do I sound too confident? To be honest, some of the credit should go to social media and a few college computer programming classes.

Once I have a name, I'm untouchable. While the commoners are drifting off to sleep, I'm locked on my computer screen learning everything available about that person.

Is it weird? Yes. Psychotic? Without a doubt. Effective? Of course.

After an introduction and brief research, I can become the exact person they want me to be. People don't care who I truly am, they're only focused on the way they want to see me.

Jeff Douglas lives a boring and unsatisfied life, from what I do know about him, but who am I to judge his lifestyle?

I could expose his extramarital affair, but what would that do for me?

I never understood the concept of "cheating." A person can want to be with someone, but drift off to other people as long as they come back to the person they want to be with.

People don't see it that way. If there is one fault all of us have, it's that we want an absolute commitment from the people closest to us.

The idea of monogamy is an archaic idea. It developed out of necessity for hunter gathers because of food. A man couldn't kill a deer and feed eight children from four different women. Humans have adapted, but why haven't we ridden ourselves of this ancient ideology?

The Destruction of a Psychopath by an American Beauty

Yet I understand it. We want to be chosen first, and not just once, but every time.

I'm a loyal person, but I also understand I prioritize myself and my own satisfaction over everyone else. I make decisions based on what is best for me because it's what everyone does.

When it comes down to it, we are all selfish people doing unselfish things for selfish reasons. No one volunteers to build a home for a refugee family because they enjoy building homes for refugee families. People build homes for refugee families to feel good about themselves, maybe even brag about it in the office or at a family cookout.

When I was in school, it was mandatory for students to complete 10 hours of community service every six weeks.

I always did, but of course, I had ulterior motives. I attended the service projects where the best-looking girls volunteered and completed the hours simply because it was required to graduate.

We aren't born with good or bad bones in our body, but we do have selfish bones. We make decisions that will most positively impact our lives because we want to improve our own reputations in society.

I don't fault anyone for making a decision that benefits them. It's what I do. It's what everyone does but at least I'm able to admit it.

I've told girls I've dated that I don't mind if they "cheat" on me. They all scoff at the notion, but marriage in the 21st century could be a much happier place if everyone was willing to open their relationships.

35

Marriage is the one of the scariest things in life. It's so absolute. How can you really know that you're making the right choice?

People spend time searching for the one perfect person for them, and then as soon as they think they've found them, boom, they close the deal.

Who is to say the "right person" isn't a few years down the road?

To spend the rest of your life with one person seems too restrictive. People in monotonous lives often don't reflect happiness. The first few months and even years of a marriage can be great, the shared experience of raising a child can be memorable, but what happens when old age arrives?

Is sex the defining factor in every relationship? If you don't have sex, it's just a friendship; if you have sex with other people, should your partner find out, you will no longer be in the relationship. Infidelity is possible, and if you're smart, you can cover it up.

Jeff Douglas has hidden his adultery well, but I uncovered it. Who else will?

Georgia Brooks is climbing the corporate ladder and a messy affair is the first thing that could destroy her career. Add that with her three-year relationship with her boyfriend and she could face being labeled a "cheater." Douglas has plenty to lose as well, a happily bored wife, a family and a good job with promotions in sight.

Jeff Douglas and Georgia Brooks must realize how much is at stake. If either one comes clean to their significant other, they're nearly guaranteed mutually-assured destruction, similar to the

Cold War. Both of their lives will come crashing down when the first one cracks.

I think Douglas will. He's weak enough to give into guilt. Eventually, it'll eat away at him, an acidic beast that destroys from the inside.

Douglas doesn't realize he has it all at this exact moment and it will come crashing down eventually. He doesn't have the mental ability to enjoy what he has in the moment.

We all give in to the temptation of looking backward or forward, failing to focus on the present. In the best and worst moments of our lives, we are rarely able to evaluate their importance as they occur. We need time to process and place meaning on those moments in our lives. That's frustrating for most people and they get the feeling that time slipped through their fingers.

It's not a problem for me. I can foreshadow the future and connect the past, while remaining relevant in the present. Every moment can be a singular event for me, which I break into its own capsule, valuing everything for what it would be, what it is, and what it was. I'm able to gauge every moment of my life for how significant or unremarkable it is.

I think the clarity is a gift, but then again, it makes me feel like everything is ordinary.

When I was younger, things seemed so much more important. A game of Little League baseball shook the world, a great grade on a test went down in history. No pun intended.

But the older I got, the more I realized none of it truly mattered. Everything felt meaningless; fate was inevitable. I feel so small and useless.

But tonight I'm the master of Jeff Douglas's life. I know more about him than he does and certainly more than his wife does. If only she was smart enough to cross reference her husband's credit card purchases with Georgia's Instagram stories.

Does she ever lay beside him at night and wonder about the person he is? Does she even want to know? No one wants to know.

Seeking the truth becomes so engrained in our heads that we hold tight to the people we're closest to, but do we ever truly and fully know who someone else is?

What we see in them is what we want to see.

I shouldn't know all of this about Douglas's life, and while I may remember it, I return the wallet and walk away from his life, my dark knowledge of his secrets slowly slipping out of the forefront of my attention.

Our lives are private and should not be shared with just anyone. Unless of course, it's our thousands of followers on social media.

If we get a distorted reality of someone on social media and an altered perspective of them in real life because of our own ideas of who they are, what exactly is the absolute truth about that person?

6

On Monday morning, Jason woke up at 6:45 a.m. to start his work week.

He was entertained by seeing people rush to their 8-5 jobs, never realizing he faced the same exact routine. He denied the mundane quality of a repetitive life by assuring himself he was a step beyond the white-collar workers dedicated to their schedule.

He believed his career was an insignificant part of his life, so being on time for work on a Monday in August meant little to him. Jason's dispassion for his job didn't translate to his behavior, though. In his three years at Creative Productions, a regional advertising agency with branches in four metropolitan areas, Jason always showed up at least 15 minutes early to work.

Jason worked as a creative account associate, yet when he first entered the work force, he hadn't set out to pursue that specific position. In fact, he fell into it.

With a creative mind built for writing, Jason was attracted to advertising when he was in college. His ability to manipulate desire and reach the attention of the target market made him a good fit for the marketing field. And after six months at

Creative Productions, Jason proved he was more than an imitator. He had a natural gift.

At 25 years old, Jason was the youngest associate to handle a national account and he had a growing reputation in the local industry. Often, he'd be called into meetings and asked questions by people twice his age who made four times his salary.

Unlike most people in his office, Jason could read and predict what people wanted to hear, which. helped him create seamless ads for clients. He knew what drew the target demographic's attention, so it didn't take long before his supervisors recognized his talent.

While people were left in awe, Jason grew easily bored with assignments he was given. He wasn't assertive within the company, didn't ask for promotions or raises and he was unwilling to network with colleagues. It was hard for him to generate any excitement for himself about the field he was working in, primarily because it wasn't a challenge.

He believed himself to be the most talented ad man in the region, but thought of it as useless. In Jason's mind, work, school, love and life all were meaningless in the shadow of the inevitable outcome everyone faced. The corporate world helped reaffirm this belief.

Jason remembered reading an obituary of an ad man in Louisville when he first started at Creative Productions. It listed the man's years of work, his awards and surviving family, but Jason wanted more information. From his perspective, there wasn't enough variation and freedom in corporate America to justify spending an entire life in one place.

He noticed dulling habits of his coworkers long before it was a thought in their minds. He believed the corporate world was lost in a transient gaze of droning routines – routines he did his best to avoid.

White dress shirt, navy and red striped tie, grey pants, it must be Monday.

"Jason, how's the Farm Bureau account coming along?"

"Ready," Jason answered, shocked out of internal musings by his supervisor's question. "They're coming in today at 11 for paperwork, approval and signing."

Stanberry legitimately fears me.

Rick Stanberry, the creative director for Louisville's branch, hired Jason three years ago. Yet, over the years, Jason had proven himself to be more of a professional threat to Stanberry's job than a mentee. Had he have known more about Jason when he gave him the position, Stanberry might not have let him in the building.

Thirty years Jason's senior, Stanberry feared a phone call from the higher-ups saying Jason Vaughn was replacing him, Jason thought.

No such call had ever come, but both knew it would inevitably come someday. The anticipation itself created a silent competition between the two which only grew over time.

I'm younger, smarter, more attractive and more popular than Stanberry. I'm everything he should be, just three decades younger.

Stanberry's dull brown hair was beginning to turn grey

while a small belly began to protrude from a once tall and slim figure. Jason had never seen Stanberry without his glasses, which included photos of his entire family that were proudly displayed around his office. Stanberry was also consistent in acting passive-aggressively toward Jason, and vice versa, yet neither had enough leverage to take the other one down.

Farm Bureau was a Stanberry-led account for eight years, so Jason's recent encroachment on Stanberry's territory elevated their competition even further.

A few minutes before 11 a.m., Chief Operating Officer Bill Hunt and Marketing Director Gary Craig of Farm Bureau, walked into the lobby of Creative Productions. Stanberry rushed to meet them at the receptionist's desk.

Jason didn't like the formalities of business greetings, so he walked to the conference room as the other three joined him, chatting. After several minutes of small talk, which Jason remained quiet for, Jason discussed the advertising plans.

"We liked both of your proposals, but we're going to go with the second one," Craig said.

Dammit.

A smile grew on Stanberry's face as he glanced at Jason.

"We thought it was our best one as well, so let's talk market distribution," Stanberry said.

Jason heard voices continuing the conversation, but he'd already tuned them out. He just wanted to leave.

How could they pick Stanberry's proposal over mine?

"Does that sound right to you, Jason?" Stanberry asked smugly, pulling Jason back into the moment.

"Yes, exactly what I was thinking."

Stanberry needed something to go right in his downward spiraling life, but not at my expense. Everyone needs a win, but no one wants to sacrifice a loss for someone else's gain. Especially his.

As the four concluded the meeting, Jason trudged back to his desk as Stanberry escorted the guests to the elevator. Jason knew it wouldn't be long until Stanberry would be back at his desk to flaunt the small victory.

If I can slip to the restroom, I can avoid him until after lunch.

Jason's idea didn't work. Stanberry was still at the receptionist's desk, blocking the entrance to the restroom.

He's going to grill me in front of everyone.

"Don't worry about it bud, you can't win them all. I'll carry the bag on this one," Stanberry chuckled, slapping Jason on the shoulder.

In front of everyone.

Jason shook his head and turned the bathroom door, escaping coworkers who he believed were laughing at his expense. They weren't.

His face felt hot as he walked into the bathroom. A coworker washing his hands glanced over at Jason.

"Hey Jason, what's up man? You have to hear about my weekend."

"Well…" Jason paused, unsure of how to respond.

Jason couldn't turn on any of his characters, couldn't retrieve any of his personas to mask his current anger. His charm and illusion weren't available when he was embarrassed and frustrated, which only served to anger him more.

His coworker took Jason's feeble response as a queue to continue talking, which he did. Jason stared blankly at the man. Jason didn't plaster any false expressions onto his face, his eyes didn't light up. As his coworker continued to tell a story, Jason remained expressionless and empty.

After washing his hands, Jason and the coworker walked out of the bathroom. Jason's face felt hotter before, and his inability to falsify his interest infuriated him more. At the elevator, his coworker parted ways, offering Jason a temporary relief.

"I'll finish the story later, Jason, see ya."

Jason threw his head back in disgust while the elevator started its descent.

"If you pretend you're on a phone call, they'll stop talking to you."

"What?" Jason muttered.

He turned to the woman in the elevator, and she was looking at him.

"People don't want to be ignored, you have to give them a reason why you can't listen…Now, I'm going to hit the tenth floor, so you don't have to go all the way down. He won't be there when you get back up."

Jason smiled and nodded, feeling his emotions returning to normal.

"I couldn't have looked that distressed if I tried."

"You wouldn't have escaped on an elevator if you weren't."

The elevator doors opened on the tenth floor and Jason slowly walked out.

"Who are you?" Jason asked, turning back to the woman on the elevator.

As the doors were closing, she said, "I'll be seeing you on the elevator again, I'm sure."

With a mix of confusion and relief, Jason waited for another elevator to return him to his office floor. When he reached the lobby of Creative Productions, he had forgotten what had made him so worked up in the first place.

He sat at his desk and noticed an email from James Downing, the Operating Director of the Louisville regional branch.

'Be in my office at 1 p.m.' was the subject title, no content.

Downing was a floor above Jason and held plenty of clout that comes along with being an operating director of a regional firm. Downing had a company car, a corner office and wore $10,000 suits to work every day. Everyone seemed to revere Downing, but Jason had never been impressed by his boss's boss.

Downing had seemed simply average to him in their brief encounters. He had spoken to Downing twice in his three years along with several "good mornings."

Jason wasn't sure why Downing needed to see him. Jason worked in the creative team Downing supervised, but he didn't know anyone under 40 years-old that had been summoned to Downing's office in this fashion.

Jason canceled his lunch with Keshawn, who worked nearby, and went to Downing's office a few minutes before 1 p.m.

A suit wearer's appearance should not change as the day goes along. I look the same way as I do in the mirror in the morning as I do leaving the building in the evening.

Jason walked to Downing's administrative assistant's desk who was surprised to see a young face for the meeting. The assistant walked him into the room. "Jason Vaughn, just the man I wanted to see," Downing said as Jason walked in, "Come in, take a seat."

With precisely combed white hair, a clean-shaven face and glasses that hung below his eyes, Downing was simple and direct in communicating his ideas.

"We're competing with seven other firms for Audi's advertising budget in America. We're a big enough firm to compete for it, but I want us to land the account. We have plenty of talent, we have some of the best marketers in the area, but we don't have room for mistakes with this client," Downing continued.

"What we need now is someone with a gift, someone who didn't learn this in a classroom or from years of experience, but just has it already. I kept asking around everywhere, and your name was consistent in all of the suggestions. I've looked at your work, and you've got talent, son. I want your help on this project."

The opportunity surprised Jason. He had never worked on a national proposal before.

Let's feed his ego a little bit.

"It'd be such an honor, Mr. Downing," Jason responded. "When do I need to start preparing?"

"I've compiled a task force, there are six of us. We'll meet next Monday morning and will spend a month or so getting everything pulled together."

"All right, that's great."

"This is a big step for you, especially at your age. I'll have Neal notify accounting. You're going to see a payroll bump for this project but I need you to bring your best. You haven't been through anything like this before."

"Thank you so much for this opportunity sir, I'll see you Monday."

Jason left Downing's office, heading toward the elevator. Even this surprising advancement in his career left him unsatisfied. *If I can't be excited for this, what am I living for?* he thought.

When he reached his desk, he had almost managed to forget his interaction with Stanberry earlier in the morning. Certainly no one else remembered his failure. No, they were all still gossiping from leftover lunch conversations. He wasn't sure what lay ahead for him. Jason sat down next to a blank white board with a few hours left before he could leave.

7

*H*er skin warmed as she walked down a city sidewalk under the midday sun. She remembered walking with her mother as a child, her mom's heels click against concrete, a strong sound giving warning to everyone around.

Naomi remembered looking up at her mother, as she walked several steps behind her, seeing her strength and power she possessed. Her mother never wavered from a straight line, never dropped her direct stare at the next destination.

Naomi stepped down shallow stairs into the basement of a restaurant called Calico's. The establishment had existed in downtown Louisville for nearly a century while its patrons changed and aged with time, the restaurant itself was nearly the same since Naomi first visited with her mother as a child.

The dimly lit dining area ran parallel to a bar with stools that were often manned by the same patrons as the previous day. Naomi took a small table in the front corner and looked out a small nearby window facing the outside stairs.

She ordered an iced tea and looked around the restaurant that was typically filled with lawyers. As a child, Naomi would sit quietly, watching her mother walk around the tables to chat with other lawyers. She thought of how her mother always seemed to control each conversation she chose to engage in.

A cleaned shaved man in his early 30s unbuttoned his navy suit and walked toward Naomi.

"Have I seen you in here before?"

"Isn't that a better question for your memory?" Naomi asked.

"Well, if I asked my memory that, I wouldn't have a reason to talk to you."

"So beyond mediocre observation skills, you need a reason to do something you want?" Naomi said, as the man delicately sat on the edge of the other chair at the table.

"Well, I'm—"

"I know who you are," Naomi cut in. "Bryan Cutler, the best up-and-coming lawyer under 35 at Stein & Harrison according to Business Weekly."

Bryan smiled.

"When did you read that?"

"You're asking the wrong question," Naomi answered.

"Oh," as Bryan's faced smirked as his eyes lit up. "What should I be asking?"

Naomi leaned close to him and gently placed her hand on his thigh below the table.

"You should be asking why I'm under the assumption that you're meeting with Ross & Weber's managing partner Andy Trenton," she whispered.

"How'd you...?" Bryan trailed off.

"He just walked in," Naomi said.

Bryan turned to see Trenton pull out a barstool next to where Bryan had been sitting.

"I wouldn't keep him waiting if I were you, I hear he values punctuality," Naomi said. "Oh…and instead of trying to hit on girls at Calico's during lunch, maybe find a better venue for secret meetings you don't want your current firm to know about."

Bryan sheepishly scoffed and turned away to the bar toward Trenton.

Naomi smiled as her iced tea was delivered to the table.

A portly older man with white hair trudged down the stairs as Bryan walked to Trenton. He smiled with assurance upon seeing Naomi at the corner table.

He placed his briefcase on the table and took the seat Bryan vacated.

"So now I have to compete with that prick?" He said with a brimming smile, pointing at Bryan.

"No Clarence," Naomi said, smirking. "You know I'm a one-lawyer girl."

Clarence Kline and Naomi's mother had worked for decades building their own law firm. While Naomi's mother had retired years prior, Clarence still took on cases for the small firm. Naomi grew up around the practice and learned about practicing law through firsthand exposure. She was essentially a paralegal for her mother's firm in college and was prepared to go to law school, but a hiring agency offered her a lucrative position she couldn't turn down. She still had a hunger to practice law, so she worked with Clarence occasionally on cases. He was old and tired, and Naomi knew it. Her case strategies, legal research and ideas were the only thing keeping Clarence a successful lawyer. But no one had to know it; he'd been like a father to her, so she gladly helped.

"Case documents," Clarence said, shuffling files across the table.

"Did you request for a TRO?" Naomi asked.

"Of course," Clarence said. "I'm not in a nursing home just yet, Naomi."

"Say that again when you're walking up those stairs," Naomi smiled.

"Better be careful, I haven't paid you yet. You insult an old man too much, he might just forget."

"Just like he forgets how to show up on time," Naomi answered.

Clarence laughed and handed Naomi money under the table, which she slid into her purse.

"You know the firm would pay for you to go to law school. We wouldn't tell her. She'd be so proud."

"Why would I go to law school for three years when I'm already a lawyer?"

Clarence smiled and carefully stood up.

"You know what I used to always tell her?" Clarence asked. "I'd tell her your favorite word was 'why'. Naomi, the little girl who doesn't care about 'what' only 'why.'"

He picked up his brief case and opened the door, and began hobbling up the stairs.

Naomi gathered the cases files and made sure Bryan

Cutler made eye contact with her as she left. She wanted him to walk back to his law firm in fear that some woman might spread rumors about meeting with Trenton. She wouldn't, but he didn't know that.

She checked her phone.

Two texts from Brandon. She didn't want to respond.

She thought of how little Brandon and her friends knew about her.

She wondered why that was, but quickly realized it was because they never asked 'why?'

8

*J*ason wanted to spend Wednesday night scrolling through social media for useless information, but he agreed to go with Megan to the State Fair. He didn't like the large crowds that filled the Exposition Center and surrounding areas, but he hoped to uncover more about Megan's roommate.

When she initially asked Jason about going, he tried using subtle hints to inspire Megan into inviting her roommates.

"It's always fun to go with a group," he said after first agreeing to the outing.

"Should we see if anyone else wants to join us?" he tried a second time.

Yet, when Jason pulled into the driveway parallel to the yellow brick house, only Megan stepped outside.

"I'm so excited to do something," Megan said as she buckled into the passenger seat. "I've been bored all week and my roommates are all out of town."

A wasted night.

The two parked on a grassy hill and made their way toward the crowd. Music from a concert blared in the background.

People don't know how to enjoy concerts anymore. They're

too busy posting videos on Snapchat and Instagram to appreciate the artist. And forget about clapping, no one can do that with a phone in one hand.

When the two reached the main thoroughfare, Jason's eyes raced around the crowd. He wanted to see every person he might know that could pin him and Megan together. He had several reasons in mind to justify their date.

He wasn't embarrassed to be seen with her per say, but he just wasn't quite sure what people would think about the two of them together. The opinions of others worried him even though the predominant portion of the crowd was families and teenagers.

Jason looked upon youthful faces that were just weeks away from returning to school and remembered his days in high school.

Though he 'd been invited to the State Fair numerous times throughout the years, it was the first time he'd actually attended since he was a child. He remembered enough to comfortably lead Megan around exhibits and animals as if he had attended every year.

After viewing oversized pumpkins, award winning pigs and the state's best baked goods, Megan asked the inevitable question Jason feared.

"Want to get some food?"

Jason was health conscious, and though he would occasionally indulge himself, State Fair food wasn't exactly how he liked to splurge.

Grease dipped corn dogs and funnel cakes blanketed in sugar.

She's going to turn her slender figure into a bowling ball if she's not careful.

Megan ventured toward the food trucks and came back with a large turkey leg while Jason settled for a basket of fried chicken strips.

She looks ridiculous eating that, but she's still a little adorable.

"You look absolutely ridiculous," Jason said, smirking though not trying to hide his opinion.

Megan looked up and laughed, it was the first bit of genuine affection Jason had given her.

After the two finished eating, they walked to the Midway to play carnival games.

Jason had little trouble comprehending what Megan desired, so he assumed that she'd ask him to win her a stuffed animal. He spotted a plush creature that she might soon be begging for, but then felt a quick jab on his right shoulder.

"Used to be nobody could sneak up on Jason Vaughn."

Keshawn playfully squared up to start a mock fight and Jason went along with it for a few seconds. Keshawn then tagged Jason on the shoulder playfully, and invited the two to join him and his date.

Jason didn't think the girl Keshawn was with as attractive as Megan, so he didn't worry about his friend's judgment as the introductions began.

Distracted by the encounter with new people, Megan's eyes never connected with the prize Jason had predicted to draw her interest. Though he felt frustrated his projection was incorrect, he was more comfortable walking around with

Keshawn. People wouldn't as easily suspect him to be with Megan while he was with a group of four.

Jason didn't like thinking about it, but Keshawn was the closest thing he had to a best friend.

The two friends had met in college and paired well together. Jason didn't bother Keshawn with his deeper thoughts, but also avoided his fake personas around him. They spent time together in the same social circles and developed a friendship based on commonality.

Keshawn's personality often complimented whoever he was around, but he connected with Jason because he appreciated the subtle nuances. Jason was genuine with Keshawn – at least more genuine than he was with anyone else – and they had fun when they were together.

As they walked around the fair, Jason started an observational commentary that kept everyone laughing. Jason liked watching people and creatively assuming details about their lives but enjoyed it even more so when it brought entertainment to others. It was humorous and light-hearted joking. Jason rarely crossed an inappropriate boundary, but said enough detailed information to make the listeners believe he knew something about the target they didn't.

They were walking outside the Exposition Center when Jason saw his newest target and pointed subtly so the other three could follow along.

"On Father's Day his daughter bought him an oversized green golf shirt, this is the first time he has worn it. He's had the khaki shorts had for 10 years, held up by a belt he bought in college that he won't give up. His wife protested, but he wore white tube socks with penny loafers because he thought it would be comfortable. All he wanted to do was eat a corn dog in peace, but his wife made him go through the art exhibit again, which he escaped by saying he needed to go to the bathroom."

The group laughed as they continued to walk around.

The crowd had started to thin out, so the four decided to make their way back to the cars. The conversation went silent and Jason could tell Keshawn was priming to tell a story.

"Megan, has Jason ever told you about the time he chopped down a tree?"

"Unfortunately, not yet," Megan smiled.

"K, she doesn't need to hear this one," Jason said.

"I think I do," Megan answered.

"We're at a house party in the fall and there is this bonfire outside. It's getting low and there isn't much wood left, so this girl says, 'We ought to put it out since we're running out of wood.' Being the party boy he is, Jason valiantly says, 'No, the party must go on.' And he walks into the garage and comes out with an axe. We're all laughing, but his face is dead serious."

"I think she gets the point," Jason said.

"Keep going," Megan demanded.

Keshawn continued, "So he walks into the woods and no one sees him for 20 minutes. Then suddenly, this dude comes out of the woods lugging this tree branch yelling 'The party goes on.' Everyone starts cheering, and the bonfire keeps blazing."

Megan and Keshawn's date started laughing.

"I was just getting so bored of you guys," Jason said. "Chopping down a tree was more fun than spending more time with that company."

Jason appreciated the moments he spent with Keshawn, but could never verbally express it to his friend. He'd heard Keshawn introduce Jason as his best friend and a feeling of pride would fill Jason for a moment. Jason considered himself well-liked, but he rarely garnered enough affection for someone to admit their attachment to him.

He realized he had to be at work in seven hours as he drove Megan back to the yellow brick house.

Please don't.

"Would you like to come inside for a moment?"

No. Not in the least bit.

Jason caught himself when he noticed two cars parked in the driveway.

"Oh, sure."

He hoped Megan's roommates would be back. More specifically, one roommate in particular.

Megan walked to the kitchen for a drink while Jason waited in the living room. The house was quiet. Jason assumed everyone else in the house was already asleep.

The two talked for a few minutes and then walked upstairs to Megan's bedroom.

She undressed herself and he turned out the lights.

Afterwards, Jason began to dress himself. Megan asked

him to stay the night, but he wanted to prepare for work the next morning.

For a second time in the yellow brick house, Jason walked down the stairs followed by Megan.

When he reached the foot of the stairs, his body was flooded with nerves. The same rush he felt nights earlier had returned.

He saw her.

She was standing in the kitchen, looking out the window, wearing a white V-neck t-shirt sipping on a glass of water. She looked elegant. He paused, staring, but she disappeared from his sight as she walked onto the back patio.

He was tempted to divulge his infatuation of her to Megan, but Jason could only manage to whisper one question.

"Who's that?"

Megan opened the front door and responded, "Brooklyn, one of my roommates. Brooklyn Turner."

Jason walked to his car and drove into the darkened twilight with a name he wouldn't forget ringing in his head.

Brooklyn Turner.

9

She awoke to the sun squinting through the white curtains in an empty hotel room.

A text message from her boyfriend wishing her a good morning awaited as she gently pulled off the white sheets. She smiled blissfully, laid down her phone and prepared for the day.

After packing her small bag, she drove to her final day of the Southeast Association of Pharmaceutical Sales Convention in Atlanta.

In her soft yellow dress, she interacted with everyone she could.

It was her third year representing Buchanan Pharmaceutical, a regional pharmaceutical sales company based in Louisville.

Three long days of networking, handshakes and hundreds of brief conversations at an Atlanta conference had worn her down, but no one else could see it. She wouldn't let them.

The final minutes of the last day ticked away, and her vibrant smile remained just as strong as when she arrived Monday morning. She said her final goodbyes and handed out her final stack of business cards, then went to the parking lot so she could return home.

Before she reached the car, an older woman with a knitted blouse waved to her. She remembered meeting her on the first day.

"Honey, I've been meaning to ask you all week, how do you look so flawless?" The woman chuckled.

"With a smile and positive attitude."

"You're such a doll," the older woman said. "You ought to give my granddaughter some lessons. The energy you have, it just spreads like wildfire to everyone around you."

"Thank you so much, that's sweet of you to say."

"You're from Louisville, right? Well, I'll let you get on the road," the older woman said as she walked away.

Louisville had been her home throughout her life. She grew up in an upper-class family in the east end of the city, attending private schools.

Her natural beauty had always overshadowed her rather sincere and simple personality. Things always seemed to go her way, which made her worry people perceived it to be because of her physical appearance. She wanted to share her mind, thoughts and insecurities, but people rarely gave her the opportunity to because they were more focused on her smile, genuine nature and attractiveness.

She enjoyed her job and liked meeting new people. She tried to see the best in everyone and made it a point to learn at least one thing from each person she met.

As she drove past Nashville, her boyfriend called. She spoke with him for 73 minutes.

They met their freshmen year of college and had been

dating ever since. He was from Cincinnati and had studied to become an electrical engineer when he came to Louisville for college. They both had reached the point as young professionals when career advancement meant the possibility of relocation.

Through all of it, though, they had stayed in Louisville and stayed together. She loved him, but never thought of herself as dependent on him. She had frequently told him that if the right opportunity were to come along, she would move away from Louisville to advance her career. She knew he would follow her.

The miles passed by as the two continued to talk, her smile and laughs filled the car as she drove closer to home. She remembered their dinner to celebrate their one-year anniversary – the same night she realized she could foresee a future with him more permanently by her side, a thought that had yet to fade.

It would be too late to see him tonight, but she asked him to spend a night with her family before the conversation ended. Her family had become as comfortable with him as they were with their own son. The family knew that a proposal, engagement, marriage and a son-in-law was assured.

For six years, she had been in love with him and had no doubt that would change. He treated her with respect and kindness. He was everything she wanted in a partner.

With darkness blanketing the sky, she pulled into her driveway and walked into her quiet house. She had lived there for a few years with her college friends, but in a few weeks, she planned to move into her boyfriend's apartment.

The two planned to buy a house together soon after it. She believed the house would come along with his proposal. She was ready for it, and so was he.

She grabbed her small bag from the trunk and walked into a dark house. Her three roommates were gone, so she turned on a few lights. She tossed her heels in the closet and took a shower before getting ready for bed.

After slipping on a white V-neck t-shirt, she lay in her bed, skimming through a French novel. She wanted to learn the language so she could walk the streets of Paris confidently speaking French. She wanted to examine every painting in the Louvre, envisioning every brush stoke each artist took to complete the masterpiece. She wanted to travel in order to expand her experience and change her perspective but had yet to find the time.

The front door creaked opened and faint voices filled the living room. A few minutes later, the voices disappeared upstairs.

After struggling to read a chapter of the novel, she headed to the kitchen for a glass of water before she went to sleep. She walked down the long hallway into the kitchen and poured water in a glass as she leaned back on the countertop.

Footsteps softly sounded down the stairs. It was the same young man that was at the house on Saturday night. She heard him pause at the foot of the stairs, but she was more focused on the sun setting outside, lighting the sky on fire.

She had often admired the sunrise and sunset through her

kitchen window, but had missed both for the past three days. She stepped onto the back patio to gaze at the colorful sky.

She glanced inside as Megan, one of her three roommates, opened the front door for him.

After the brief disruption, she looked at the night sky sprinkled with stars, the dark chasing the trails of yellow and orange to the horizon. She felt so small and incapable, even though she had everything she wanted. The endlessness of the sky above her was vaster than her future.

What else was there for her to want? she thought.

10

The heat of the summer sun had already begun to roast the pavement when Jason stepped outside of his apartment on Monday morning. He could handle winter cold and the spring rain, but the steamy months of July and August were unbearable. The short walk from his car to the office was even too hot.

Often, he sat in his office chair fearing the sweat that would inevitably drip down his neck soon after he left the safety of the building's air-conditioning. He always avoided being outside in summer heat for too long, but humid sweat remained a constant worry anytime the temperature rose to 90 degrees.

He sat at his desk knowing this Monday would be different. He planned to make his way upstairs to the conference room where he would spend the next six weeks working on Audi with Creative Production's brightest minds.

Before he left his desk, he watched his coworkers rush into the office to begin their mundane work week on time.

A mere 40 hours of drudgery sits between them and a few days of relief. And then they waste their days off watching television shows and checking social media. Are they pretending their weekends are better than the weekdays?

Jason's coworkers had showered him with compliments and jealousy when they learned of his opportunity to work on the Audi project. The assignment didn't feel extraordinary to him as he considered the only difference to be reporting to another floor.

He hadn't shared the news with anyone that didn't ask about it. He didn't feel the need to hide it, but he didn't see a reason to share it with everyone, either.

Jason caught the elevator to the 28th floor and then made his way to the designated conference room, which was beginning to fill with people. When he entered the room, everyone turned to look at him. More than two decades younger than everyone else, Jason's presence had the room's curiosity.

To regain his presence and authority, James Downing cleared his throat and introduced Jason in his thick voice.

"Everyone, this is Jason Vaughn, the final piece to our team. He's going to provide the spark we need for this project."

I don't need an introduction.

The four other members on the Audi team already knew him. When they heard a 25-year-old associate was assigned to the project, they demanded to see some of his past projects. After 20 minutes of seeing his creative work, they realized they might actually learn a bit from him.

Their only chance of winning the struggle of creative minds was to overwhelm him early, forcing the younger, less experienced man to feel uncomfortable and unwelcomed.

What the four didn't know was that Jason already thought he was better than them, and if anyone would be overwhelmed, it would be them.

Yet, regardless of the potential competition of ideas, the six-member team was the best group Creative Productions could assemble. Downing had done a good job bringing in a good mix of talent.

George Profitt had worked in the industry for 30 years and traveled from the Chicago branch for the project. He was short, black-haired and a plain-spoken man.

Kathy Wiseman brought two decades of experience from St. Louis. Jason thought she looked better suited to be a librarian.

Caroline Trout and Michael Davies, national creative account managers from Louisville, were the final members of the team.

Downing spent the first hour of the meeting discussing the bid proposal from Audi and covering the competition the team faced. As eyes rolled with discontent about other advertising agencies, Jason focused on what would come next.

He didn't know any of the competitors. And he didn't want to.

Advertising is about the best thing that can be created by an individual; it's not firms competing against each other. If I have the best idea, my idea will get chosen.

Despite his discontent with the industry, Jason's ideas had been selected more times than not in his young career.

Once Downing finished the introductory briefing, the

six members began to openly discuss what needed to be done. Downing refrained from becoming too involved in the conversation, listening to his team converse and already allowing ideas to bounce back and forth.

The team had two weeks before its first meeting with Audi representatives. They had access to a pool of Creative Productions' associates for market research and studies.

Jason preferred to study and search on his own. The research helped bury him in the project and focus his mind as he waited for a moment of brilliance surrounded in paperwork.

He stayed quiet during the morning meeting that ran past noon, simply observing and playing the role of a humble young associate. The team stopped for lunch around 12:30. Everyone left the room under-impressed by the young ad genius.

Jason retreated to his desk and then headed to meet Keshawn for lunch. The two walked a block over to Subway and waited in line during the lunch rush.

Unlike others in line at the restaurant, Jason wasn't bothered by waiting in lines. He was humored by people who rushed through red lights or impatiently bickered at a store clerk for taking too long.

The difference in 30 seconds isn't going to make a marketable difference in their lives, so why complain about something that will be irrelevant in ten minutes? People want to rush to the next destination, but what are they really rushing too?

Keshawn usually talked about his job during lunch, so Jason would listen, but rarely interjected about his own responsibilities. Even though the two were close friends, Keshawn couldn't accurately say what Jason did at work.

"What else did Megan and you do this weekend?"

Jason purposefully avoided conversations about his personal life, even with his close friends, but decided to answer to prevent any more questions.

Jason explained how he and Megan went to Circle's on Friday night with Julie, Kyle, Brandon and Naomi. He brought her back to his apartment for the night and they spent time together on Saturday. Despite his insistence on going to her house Sunday night with the hopes of catching a glimpse of Brooklyn again, Megan came to Jason's apartment for a few hours.

"You're moving fast with this girl man. I'll need to start planning a bachelor's party."

"Who said you'd get invited?" Jason responded.

"If you didn't invite me, you wouldn't have anyone there," Keshawn said.

The two laughed, but Jason couldn't help but agree with Keshawn's joke.

"It's not serious though. We've only seen each other a few times," Jason said.

"You like her?"

Why does everyone have to ask that question? When I was in middle school, my friends used to ask me who I liked. I never had an answer. I knew what girls were attractive, but I never had an emotional attachment to any of them.

"She's got some good qualities."

"It sounds like you're writing a review about an Amazon product," Keshawn said.

Keshawn could sense he'd badgered Jason enough about Megan, so he changed the topic.

While Jason casually spoke about Megan and time spent with her, she felt much differently. The past two weeks had further solidified her deep attraction to Jason, yet he not only failed to realize it, he also failed to feel the same way.

The sun scorched down on Jason as he walked back to the office after lunch. He felt the threat of sweat just before he was flooded by cool air in the front lobby.

As Jason walked toward the elevators, a familiar face attracted his attention.

"Any fake business calls planned this afternoon?" he was asked.

The woman Jason met in the elevator last week was waiting for her transit up to her office space.

Their last encounter was less than a minute, so Jason failed to notice how young the woman was. She looked to be in her early thirties, but retained some of the youthfulness of her twenties. She had brown hair with soft streaks of blond highlights and glasses that looked comfortable on her. She had a soft smile.

"I'm Grace; I work a few floors above you at Great American Insurance."

Even though she was just seven or eight years older than Jason, he perceived she had wisdom about her comparable to an older sister or aunt. He entered the elevator smiling, already looking forward to seeing her again.

He felt relaxed talking to Grace. They talked uninhibited until the elevator doors opened on the 27th floor. Jason was disappointed the elevator ride was ending. He started to step out to let its journey continue upward.

"I like our elevator small talk," Jason said.

"That's the thing though, I'm trying to elevate small talk to medium talk," Grace paused and smiled. "I'll be seeing you on the elevator again, I'm sure."

Jason nodded and walked to his desk to prepare for the afternoon workload.

Once back in the conference room on the floor above, the team continued to labor through initial situations for the Audi account. By 2:30, Jason was bored. His creativity was useless in such a restricted setting.

He knew the first week would be a waste of time, so he sat through the meeting and said nothing. It concluded at 5:17.

Finally, he was able to leave for the day.

As he pushed the elevator button to descend from the 28th floor, he hoped Grace would be on the elevator.

If their timing was perfect, he could listen to her insightful commentary about various office happenstances, maybe even walk with her outside to continue their enlightening dialogue.

I like what she said earlier. Why should we waste time with small talk? Let's have meaningful conversations. I don't want to listen to someone recapping their day of work. I want my intellect to be challenged, similar to the chats I have with Naomi.

The elevator doors opened to an empty cabin and Jason's hopes dropped along with the elevator.

When he reached the lobby, he paused to see where the other elevators were headed. One of the elevators was stopped on the 36th floor. He scanned the mounted directory to find that Great American Insurance on the 33rd floor.

He waited for its descent by nonchalantly tying his shoes in hopes of creating another coincidental meeting. The elevators doors opened, but Grace wasn't inside.

Disappointed, Jason walked to his car under the still steaming summer sun.

11

*A*fter a full week of work, Jason decided to join his friends at Heather's lake house for the weekend. Her parents owned a small house and a boat at the dock, allowing her friends access to it a few weekends a summer.

Jason agreed to go in hopes of escaping Megan, but Julie invited her to join them. Megan wouldn't say no to a chance to spend time with Jason for an entire weekend, as her feelings continued to develop.

After work on Friday, Jason, Keshawn, Kyle and Brandon made the two-hour drive while Julie, Heather, Naomi and Megan followed in a separate car.

Jason typically liked to drive his friends to assert his control over them, but he was tired tonight. He nestled in the back corner of the car and listened to incoherent banter. He didn't have the energy to critique Brandon's driving, so with little thought he rested his head against the window.

He tried to envision the conversation in the other car. He assumed the four young women were analyzing and debating Jason's every attribute. He thought Megan would be asking questions to gain a better sense of who he was when he was around his friends.

He doubted any of them would give her anything substantial simply because none of them knew him well enough despite several years of friendship. Jason knew Naomi could provide the best insight into him, but he also realized she would be the quietest in the car when he became the topic of conversation.

Jason drifted to sleep for a few moments. The setting sun was just enough in the distance for him to rest from the long work week. When he awoke, the two cars were pulling into the lake house driveway. They unloaded and prepared the house for the weekend.

An hour later, several other friends of the group who lived around the lake joined them. The dozen people crowded onto the back patio, some even braving the murky water of the infrequently cleaned pool.

Jason enjoyed the company of strangers. It allowed him to sit in the back corner of the patio and observe the interactions. He watched everyone socialize, but Megan continued to return to him to talk.

Megan's hovering around me like a house fly, I wish I could swat her away. I just want time to think.

Jason diverted his attention to anything else to avoid her constant need for interaction.

The night went on and the group continued to drink. The laughter grew louder, but the conversations became duller.

As alcohol stirred in her blood, Megan built enough courage to confront Jason.

"Why aren't you paying attention to me?"

Jason smiled and pulled her into an embrace.

"I'll do whatever you need me to do."

I don't think she can sense the insincerity. It's not always what you say, it's the way you say it. That'll keep her happy for the night.

Jason slowly drifted to sleep after everyone had retreated to beds and couches.

The next morning, everyone seemed to rise in unison to prepare for the day ahead. They carried the supplies onto the boat and departed from the dock.

Julie and Megan were talking quietly on a bench at the back of the boat, so Jason sat near the front and felt the wind whip his face as they moved into deeper water.

The boat slowed down, allowing Kyle to shout a joke that made everyone laugh.

It was then that Jason noticed Keshawn and Heather look at each other first when Kyle said the humorous comment.

In a group setting, the first person you look at when something is said is the person you feel closest too.

Jason had looked at Keshawn, but the look hadn't been returned. Jason then realized the two were together, but neither of them were comfortable enough to tell the rest of their friends.

Their secret was safe with Jason. Even though Keshawn was his closest friend, Jason wouldn't pester him about Heather.

A little before noon, the boat settled in a deep cove away from the main lake. The day was simple and slow, which Jason detested. He wanted a fast-paced life, all the time. He couldn't understand why anyone would want to spend weekends doing nothing. He could lounge on a boat for one Saturday in the summer but sacrificing every weekend for uneventful experiences seemed worthless to him.

While everyone else enjoyed each other's company, Jason floated in the water, wondering what they would do next.

Several hours later, the lake friends from the previous night pulled their boat into the cove. Jason didn't intend to be disconnected from them, but he inevitably was. He had known them for years, but he couldn't manufacture an amusing personality for them.

Once the two boats joined together, a medley of people jumped into the water. One of the guys began to talk to Megan, but Jason didn't care.

I hope he takes her. I could play the broken hearted, 'some dude stole my girl' character really well.

Jason paddled around in the water without any jealousy.

"I can swim the furthest underwater," Kyle announced to everyone, causing an uproar and initiating a competition.

No one could ever beat me.

Each took a turn diving off the front of the boat and swimming underwater. When they finally broke for air, the person in the lead would remain at their distance marker, waiting for the next to threaten their win.

When it was his turn, Jason filled his lungs with air and dove in. He glided through the water knowing no one could match his ability. When he finally surfaced and gasped for air, he was well beyond the current frontrunner.

The final man from the other boat dove in and started to

sliver through the water. As the swimmer approached him, Jason realized his mark would be surpassed.

Softly treading water, Jason inched back further. No one noticed Jason's cheating action saved his status in the game, they were all watching the swimmer, who came up just a few feet short of Jason.

Proclaimed the winner, Jason was complimented by his friends, who raved about his swimming ability.

"There isn't anything he can't do well," Julie shouted from the boat.

The sun began to set, so they decided to return to the dock. Megan rested her head on Jason and held his hand as the boat made its trip back.

Get off me. Why does she always have to be touching me? I want to throw her in the water.

Jason hid his dispassion with several jokes. She didn't seem to notice his disgust.

Words left unspoken mean more than what is often said aloud.

After the eight returned to Heather's lake house and rested for a few hours, they returned to the back patio and started drinking. Jason stared at the night sky as he listened to his friends talk.

He missed the times when he was younger, when he could drink less and feel tipsy. His thinking had become so rigid over the years that alcohol didn't do much to change his thoughts or decision-making. Jason was the exact same person with or without alcohol.

He considered this aspect about himself convenient, but it frustrated him as well. He couldn't force himself into a careless mindset that disregarded the personalities he played.

By midnight, Megan was feeling sick. Like younger Jason, Megan was easily altered by small amounts of alcohol. Jason had lost all compassion for her due to her earlier physical clinginess, so he asked if Julie would make sure she was okay.

And ever so slowly, one person at a time retired for the night until Jason was left on the patio by himself.

He walked inside and laid on the couch for a few minutes. After feeling a phantom rocking of the sea from being on the boat all day, he returned to the patio with a pen and notebook.

He started to write.

He hadn't written in months, aside from his gig at the newspaper. It felt good to put words onto paper simply for himself and no one else.

He began a short story:

She felt her hands wavering at the wheel as the fading sunlight scraped across bare fields. Her weary eyes struggled to stay open, so she looked for the nearest highway exit. Several miles down the road, she pulled into a large gas station filled with tourists and truck drivers needing a moment of reprieve.

She imagined herself as a child, with her two sisters and parents, going on a vacation trip. Though it never happened, she envisioned their minivan filled to the brim with packs and coolers, waiting to be opened at the perfect destination.

She filled her car with gas and watched people wander around the station without thought of anything except where they were going. After buying a bottle of water, she started her car again and caught in the rearview mirror a glimpse of the sun setting against the horizon.

Before driving off, she submitted to a somber smile as she spotted a car pulling to a gas pump a few spots down. It was her friend, who had so ferociously existed in her life many years ago. Yet, the inevitable passing of time threatened their relationship and eventually drove them apart. Though time is something no one can conquer, she often remembers the times they had together, how they met by accident. Her life had been shaped by coincidences; meeting him had been one of the few happy ones.

They had shared so much, so long ago, but none of it mattered now. He looked decades older and very different, yet she could still see the youthful life that she'd loved about him, hidden by years of time and age.

She watched as a woman, presumably his wife, and a child, exit the car and head inside, leaving him to the fill the car with gas. Back then, he'd known as much about her as she'd known about him, but now, they were travelers headed in different directions.

She knew he was pretending, not in the same way he once did when he'd humorously act in certain personas. She knew it was deeper than that now. She knew he had to pretend everything and hide the person he truly was. She knew his wife didn't know the entirely of the man she once knew.

He decided to turn off the genuine part of him, and she knew it would never be switched on again.

His family walked back to the car and he smiled as they

climbed in. He paused, waiting for the receipt, and, by chance, looked over at her, their two connecting eyes for a moment.

It was enough for her. He nodded and she knew what he wanted to say to her: "They'll never know who I am."

She understood and he knew she would. They would never see each other again and they both knew it. They had once separately dreamed of an emotional encounter where they'd be reunited and never be divided again. Yet now, they were 20 years older and as close as they would ever be: 18 feet away at a gas station off a highway exit.

She knew him and he knew her, and the moment they shared looking into each other's eyes was enough. She wanted more and vice versa, but they knew even love wouldn't be able to conquer time.

The pen continued to scribble under the night sky and Jason would only break for brief moments as thoughts spilled onto the pages uncontrollably.

Jason knew everyone else was asleep, but he hadn't felt this alive in a long time. He liked knowing that everyone rested quietly while he wrote. It gave him the solitude he needed to creatively compile the words flowing in his head.

He paused for a moment, staring up at the night sky once more, and realized how large all of it seemed. His writing wouldn't be stopped by the stars or his midnight reflections regarding them, though, so he continued.

He was nearly dry of thoughts and ready to go inside when the patio door opened. It had been more than two hours since everyone had gone to sleep.

Naomi stepped outside and sat down in a chair next to Jason.

"I thought you'd gone to sleep," Jason said.

"What are you writing about?" Naomi asked, ignoring his statement.

"Different things, sometimes it just all comes to me at once and I can't stop."

"You're a businessman yet you want to write. But you want money more than you want to write, so you stay a businessman," Naomi said.

Jason shrugged in agreement. Naomi sat back in her chair.

"How long did it take you to figure out about Keshawn and Heather?" she asked.

"What do you mean?" Jason asked, trying to fake innocence.

"I'm guessing today then," Naomi said. Obviously, Jason wasn't great at lying to Naomi.

"How long have you known?" Jason said.

"I didn't know until I watched you today. You started looking at them differently, you didn't joke with either of them about other people they could be pursuing and you didn't really know what to say."

"It's not my place to get into their personal lives," Jason said. "And we shouldn't go around spreading it until they say something to all of us."

"Jason, you wouldn't be talking about this with me unless you knew I wasn't going to go spreading it around."

"Wait, you knew before today, right?"

"I did."

"You just wanted my confirmation," Jason said.

"My perceptions don't need your confirmations to be correct," Naomi said.

Jason smiled and agreed with her. They looked up at the night sky. Jason slouched further down in his seat.

He realized he hadn't openly talked about Megan to anyone yet.

"I don't know what to do about Megan. She's sick and I've been out here writing all night."

"She doesn't realize it." Naomi shook her head.

Jason pressed onward and took the bait.

"She doesn't realize what?"

"Being affectionate only pushes you further away," Naomi answered.

"Is that how it's always going to be?" Jason asked, more to himself than Naomi.

Naomi stood up and said, "Probably will always be that way with her. The tougher question is if it'll always be that way with everyone?"

Jason didn't have a response, so he sat back in the chair and looked back up into the night sky.

Naomi took a towel drying on a lounge chair and draped it over Jason. She walked back inside and turned off the patio light.

Too tired to say anything, Jason glanced over and watched as she walked deeper into the dark house.

12

Jason couldn't successfully avoid Megan's persistence, so he agreed to meet her family for dinner Sunday evening after the trip to the lake house. He hadn't been nervous in years but he could feel some anxiousness in his stomach as he pulled into the driveway of the yellow brick house to pick up Megan.

He imagined himself leaving town never to return, but his vision was interrupted by Megan opening the car door.

"I'm so excited you finally get to meet them," Megan said.

It had only been a few weeks since their first date, but Megan had been taking their "relationship" much more seriously than Jason. He hadn't met a girl's family in years, so Jason went into the dinner planning to stay as quiet as possible.

Megan's parents' house in Jeffersontown was larger than Jason expected. It was two stories of grey bricks, with a well-manicured front yard and curving driveway that wrapped into the backyard and garage.

Jason could sense everyone's eyes fall upon him when he walked through the front door with Megan. Megan's older brother, his spouse and their young child sat in the open living room. Her parents, both in their late 50s, stood near the entry way that led to the kitchen.

Megan was happily greeted by everyone before they turned their attention to Jason. He watched their affection for Megan. They shared a warmness for each other that Jason wasn't accustomed to.

He was cordial and comfortable, but remained reserved, as he had planned.

"Jason, we've already heard so much about you," Megan's mother said.

She was a short woman with highlighted hair and a relatively petite figure, although the wrinkles around her eyes and worn skin didn't do well to hide her age.

Jason blended in perfectly as the six adults and young child sat down to eat. They each took their turns talking about their jobs and recent events, which allowed Jason to silently listen and observe.

"You've been awfully quiet over there Jason," Megan's father said.

Yeah, because all you guys do is talk and interrupt each other. I wouldn't be able to get a word in if I tried.

"Oh, I enjoy listening," Jason answered.

"So, what do you do?"

"I'm in advertising," Jason said.

I need to steer this conversation away from me.

"This house is wonderful, by the way, how long has your family lived here?" Jason said, turning to Megan.

And there they go.

Jason listened as Megan's mother and father retold the story of finding, purchasing and renovating the house.

After they finished eating, the family gathered around the one-year old and watched as he crawled around the floor. Jason tried to hide his disinterest as everyone else intently focused on the child. He didn't think babies were amusing or worthy of his attention.

Megan placed her hand on Jason's leg and said, "Don't you just want to pick him up and hold him?"

Jason laughed to avoid giving an honest answer.

I haven't held a child. Ever. I don't think babies are cute. I understand the physiological attraction parents have for their children, but why does it have to get pushed onto other people?

A half hour passed before everyone agreed it was time to leave. Megan guided Jason toward the front door as her parents followed them.

Jason uncomfortably hugged Megan's mother and then shook her father's hand.

"You seem like a fine young man," Megan's father said.

I don't seek or need your approval.

"Thank you, it was nice meeting you."

The sun had crept behind the horizon as the two drove back to Megan's house. After spending several hours with her family, Jason knew what Megan's question would be as his car pulled into the driveway of the yellow brick house.

"When are you going to introduce me to your family?" Megan asked.

"Oh, they aren't really in the picture," Jason said.

He hadn't seen his parents since high school. He could tell Megan that his mother was cold and his father despondent, but she wouldn't understand. She had grown up in a house filled with affection. His childhood had been defined by survival.

He wasn't beaten, abused or neglected. More than anything, he was simply forgotten. He always had food, clothes and a bed, but he shared no emotional connection with his parents. His friends in high school joked that Jason's parents were his roommates while others thought he was a foster child because his mother and father made no public appearances with him.

My parents never cared enough about my life. I was a burden more than a responsibility, but that's not something I go around saying.

"Oh, that's sad, maybe you can change that."

"I don't think so."

Megan looked down in innocent despair.

"Do you want to come inside for a little bit?" she asked.

"Not tonight," Jason said.

He watched Megan walk to the front door and wave before backing down the driveway. There was only one place he wanted to go tonight. As the twilight faded to darkness, he made his way back to his childhood home. It had been several years since he had driven by the old house in St. Matthews.

The grass was unkempt and the bushes sprawled near the one-story ranch house. He used to keep the yard finely manicured to give the appearance of a stable family living in a solid home.

He parked across the road in front of the house and looked inside the living room window from the comfort of his car. His parents still lived in the house, and his mother read by a dim light. She looked so much older than the last time Jason had seen her. He wasn't sure where his father would be.

He continued to look at the house as darkness blanketed the neighborhood. He didn't feel any pain about the relationship with his parents, but he had no positive feelings toward them either.

They had existed for the first 18 years of his life. He used them out of necessity by understanding he was an unwanted imposter in their lives.

After looking at the house where he'd spent most of his life, Jason drove back to his apartment.

He didn't know how to accept affection because he had never been around it.

13

*A*fter spending seven days mashing their heads together waiting for a creative idea strong enough to capture the attention of Audi, the Creative Productions team had officially hit a stalemate. No one had produced anything interesting, but Downing kept his underlings in the same conference room in hopes that the mutual frustration would spark an idea.

With only two weekdays left before their initial presentation, it was already assumed that the six-member team would spend their weekend hashing out ideas to formulate a respectable presentation. Tensions between the coworkers had grown, but Downing believed the hindrance would lead to an eventual break through.

Jason was miserable. The daily routine of sitting eight hours in the conference room was boring and uneventful. He looked out the window and small raindrops fell from the soft grey clouds. He knew there was activity on the streets below, but hundreds of feet above it, Jason was forgotten as the world continued to move forward.

Jason watched a plane soar off in the distant sky. He

wondered where it was headed and envied the feeling of freeness that consumed the passengers.

Kathy started complaining about a headache early in the morning. By the early afternoon, it had spread to everyone. Downing tried to diffuse the mounting struggle of the situation, but he mostly remained quiet as the group talked through the project. Downing's cell phone rang.

"Damn, I forgot, I have documents waiting downstairs that I need to sign for."

Downing looked for his assistant, but he wasn't at his desk.

Kathy spoke snidely, "Make Jason go get it."

George added on, "Yeah, he's the youngest."

"It's not like he'll be missed, the so called 'creative genius' has just sat here for two weeks like an intern, not saying anything," Kathy continued.

"That's enough," Downing said.

Instead of picking a fight, Jason slowly rose and said he would get the documents.

I'll always choose flight over fight. I know how to run from situations, escaping problems is easier than addressing them.

Avoiding problems was what he knew how to do. He wasn't frustrated by Kathy's comments either. What she said was true. He hadn't done much to impress the task force. Jason liked to have a subtle pride in his work, but for the past week-and-a-half he hadn't done anything worthwhile or productive. He wanted to prove himself and hoped for a signature moment when a perfect idea would come forward from him, but he hadn't delivered anything of substance yet.

When the door opened on the 27th floor, Stanberry joined Jason in the elevator. With his glasses hanging a little below his eyes, Stanberry was surprised to see Jason during his six-week hiatus to the 28th floor. He knew about the work he'd been excluded from, and wasn't happy about it.

"It's been a lot quieter without you. I hope you're still managing your current accounts for me."

"I am, I've been working extra hours to make sure everything is all set with them."

A lie. Stanberry comes in at 8:45 a.m. every day and leaves at 4:30 p.m., so he wouldn't even be in the office to see me working overtime even if I did put in the extra hours. Plus, managing those remedial accounts takes seconds for me. Live in the lie.

"What does Downing have you working on?"

"You asking because you want to join?" Jason prodded.

"No," Stanberry said.

"Just a few different things for preparing the pitch," Jason said.

"Oh yeah, I've been there before," Stanberry answered.

Sure you have.

While I'm lying to him, he's more so lying to himself. That's worse than what I'm doing. People lie to themselves every day to hide the reality they live.

As the elevator opened at the first floor, Jason remembered his reason for being on the elevator. He didn't want Stanberry to see him being an errand boy, so Jason walked toward a food stand to cover his real mission.

After Stanberry exited the building, Jason walked to the delivery man and signed for the package of documents.

"I apologize for taking so long, these elevators can be such a burden sometimes," Jason said.

The delivery man didn't acknowledge Jason's apology. Jason carried the awkwardly shaped package of documents back to the elevator. He noticed Grace, who was wearing a light blue sundress and standing with two of her coworkers waiting by the elevator doors.

"One minute you're an ad man, and the next, a postal boy," Grace joked.

Jason laughed, but the conversation was hindered by Grace's other two coworkers on the elevator ride.

It was the first time he had seen Grace on the elevator this week, but Jason couldn't talk the way he wanted to with her. However, their brief interaction, despite the lack of substantial conversation, was enough to motivate Jason back into the conference room for three more hours of drudgery.

The tensions had somewhat calmed in the conference room, but Jason could sense everyone was still on edge. If there was ever a moment when Downing needed to take authority of the room and lead his employees in the right direction, it was now, and Jason knew it.

Jason looked on as Downing stood in the corner of the room preparing a statement of strength and inspiration to get his task force out of its mental block.

In school, Jason had been an athletic leader, but in the past three years at Creative Productions he had worked alone.

He wasn't sure what Downing would say, because he wasn't sure what he would say himself. Even after working day after day with the task force, he felt distant. Jason tried to think of the best motivational tactic to reach the individuals in the room, but with the diverse personalities, he couldn't come to a consensus on what would work best.

"Listen to me," Downing turned and boisterously opened to his captivated audience.

He was concise and strong, like a father scolding misbehaving children. He offered no encouragement.

Jason wasn't driven or offended. His thoughts hadn't changed from before or after Downing's speech, but everyone else appeared focused.

It didn't last long. The afternoon lulled forward and nothing new was presented.

As the sun began to fall in the sky, the team members prepared to leave.

With only Kathy and Jason left in the room, she apologized for her comments earlier in the day.

Jason wasn't bothered by it and it didn't change the way he thought of her, so he briefly engaged with her and assured her it was fine.

When she finished, Jason packed his things and grabbed his umbrella that he'd used for the morning rain shower.

In the lobby, other people were filing out of the building. Jason spotted Grace's light blue dress just ahead of him and she turned several seconds later, noticing him.

"Did you finish all your deliveries?" she asked.

"I have a few more packages left in the truck," Jason said.

"You really should get a pair of shorts in these hot summer months, I can teach you how to wax your legs," Grace said.

"Women still do that…you must be older than you look," Jason joked.

"A whole wall in my house is actually filled with VHS tapes."

"That's a weird way to entice someone to visit," Jason responded.

"How about drinks then, some of my coworkers are across the street at the Underground," Grace asked.

"Not 21 yet," Jason said and the two laughed. "It's actually been a frustrating day; I'll go with you another time."

"I'll hold you to that," Grace said.

"I expect you to."

Jason left the building and walked to his car parked several blocks away. His laptop bag was strapped on his left shoulder while he carried his small wrapped umbrella in his right hand.

As Jason walked under the Second Street Bridge, a homeless man turned the corner and moved toward Jason.

Jason didn't have sympathy for homeless people. When they asked him for money, he avoided eye contact and continued walking past without responding.

The homeless man shouted for spare change as Jason moved toward him. As the two came close to crossing paths, the man reached toward Jason, who was several steps away.

Jason felt his heart beating through his chest. He raised his umbrella and swung at the homeless man, and reared back and swung again. And again. Jason delivered blows that drilled the man's neck and head, causing him to fall to the ground.

When he no longer felt threatened, Jason stood over the homeless man, watching him seethe with pain. Jason subdued the urge to continue hitting him. Jason caught himself, stepped over the beaten man and continued to his car.

Adrenaline was flowing through his body. He could feel blood circulating through his system. When he reached the car, his hands were shaking and his heart was pounding. He felt no remorse for the homeless man. He took deep breaths to calm himself. Jason felt hot, but finally regained his breath while his heart rate returned to normal. He started his car and began to drive as raindrops started to fall.

While Jason hated being unable to control his shaking and pumping heart, he. had to admit that after spending eight hours in a cycling monotony, the feeling of being alive was enough for Jason to want more.

14

When Megan asked Jason to dinner on Thursday night, he declined. It was the first time he said no to her, but after an already long week he needed time to decompress.

Jason didn't like saying no to people, believing he had the ability to do many things at once with proper time management. Though he would rush place to place, he always collected himself before he transitioned to the next stop so each commitment appeared to be his top priority.

Instead of rushing to a dinner with Megan after work and then going to the Business Weekly's office for final edits, he relaxed on Thursday evening.

He sat and exchanged text messages with Megan in his dark apartment. Jason didn't have any sense of an emotional connection with Megan, but the two were officially together. His friends knew about her and he had met her family. She posted pictures of them together on social media.

It was the first relationship Jason had since college and they'd been together for over a month.

Jason didn't feel like he was in a relationship, but the time he spent with Megan solidified the commitment. He didn't care if the relationship continued or ended – he wouldn't be emotionally affected either way.

He liked the guarantee of physical intimacy that comes with an official relationship, but he didn't need it. Megan didn't offer Jason anything that he desperately wanted. He could see her growing emotional attachment to him, but he already knew nothing would ever connect him to her.

It had been just over a month and Jason could sense the boredom overcoming his mind regarding their relationship. He hadn't grown to dislike Megan yet, but she was predictable and dull. It didn't matter that she was friendly and sincere. He needed more than her simplicity could provide.

All considered, Jason still continued his relationship with Megan. It didn't logically make sense to him to break up, though he tried to forecast how it would end.

When people are in a relationship, they never take the time to plan how it should end. In other parts of our life, we plan for retirement because we know our careers will end, we plan for death by buying cemetery plots and funeral arrangements, but in relationships we never decide how we want it to end. When relationships start, the couple should layout rules for what should happen as soon as it ends. This could prevent plenty of drama and hard feelings. And since it would be agreed upon before the collapse begins, everyone could be unemotional about it. But people don't want to accept that they will fail at a relationship before it begins. So, they go along like nothing will ever go wrong until it crumbles right in front of them.

Jason cooked rice and chicken for dinner accompanied

with a salad. He ate in his quiet and dimly lit apartment alone. He kept his apartment clean and clutter-free, but it was plain and boring. The walls were white, and even though he'd been there for three years, there was no decoration and minimal furniture. He had two plates, two bowls, several cups and a small collection of utensils in the kitchen.

He played characters and personas outside of his apartment, but when he returned, he became as plain as the walls. Almost as plain as Megan.

After meticulously washing the dishes, Jason went to the Business Weekly office in the evening twilight. He scanned his badge and walked into the empty office. Jason edited pages, breezing through articles, columns and graphics. His efficient workflow was interrupted when Ashley and Brad walked in. Both laughing, they were surprised to see Jason.

"Of course you're here tonight, I still have my work to do," Ashley said.

Jason hadn't seen Brad in months, so the two talked while Ashley placed ads on pages. Jason enjoyed talking to Brad. He was well-respected by everyone on staff. His well-groomed dark brown beard fit comfortably around a smile that seemed to be ever-present. He had a naïve positive, genuine nature.

It was a few minutes past 8:30 p.m. when Brad decided to leave. Ashley stopped her work to walk with him to his car. She was smiling to herself when she returned to the office.

"I think he's just great, he's so amazing," she said.

"Have you guys been seeing each other?" Jason asked.

"Yeah, as of a few weeks ago; he's so wonderful."

It doesn't take much for someone to become infatuated with another person. People talk about searching for the right person. If you're willing to treat someone decently, it will probably stick. How hard is it to be nice to someone? To deal with all their quirks and problems. To put on a false smile when you can't stand being with them. I could do that, anyone can. Just sit still and smile with insanity and outrage building in your head.

Ashley and Jason had spoken candidly before, so Jason wasn't surprised when she returned her thoughts to him.

"I couldn't wait for you forever, it's not like I'm replacing you or anything," Ashley said.

With a slight smile on his face, Jason responded.

"No, we wouldn't have become anything."

Ashley continued to talk, but Jason didn't comprehend a word as a deep grin cracked across his face.

He had it. Finally.

After two weeks, he could deliver the idea he wanted.

He rushed to the white board and scribbled together words and drawings.

Everything is replaceable. Our minds are set to think a certain way, social norms become standards and shape the way we think. Fine wine is considered romantic, when we think of a high-class meal, we think of steak, when we think of fast food, McDonalds comes to mind first.

These associations become ideas, and these ideas become the way we live and think. For the past few decades, luxury car brands are thought to be Mercedes Benz and Jaguar. But, everything is replaceable, including the original thought of luxury car brands.

Everything is replaceable. Audi has replaced Mercedes Benz as the luxury car brand. Audi has replaced the idea of what a luxury car is. Everything is replaceable.

Jason knew this was the creative pitch his task force needed. He drew up forms of artwork on the board, realizing he had discovered the key.

When they meet in the conference room the next morning, he'd conduct and direct what would happen. His idea for the ad pitch was original and strong. It was simple and forward.

Instead of highlighting strengths and weaknesses, the national string of advertisements would call on consumers to change the way they think. And there's nothing like trying to change the consumers' perspective that would gain more attention.

Ashley came over to the whiteboard and watched Jason.

The members of Creative Productions doubted his brilliance, but once I save the entire project, they will all realize my greatness, he thought.

Ashley continued to follow along with Jason's work on the whiteboard, so he started to rehearse his pitch to her.

Inspired by the creative idea, the morning couldn't come soon enough for Jason. He felt a nervous energy of anticipation as he turned off the lights in the office after submitting the pages for print.

The two walked across the street to the only two cars left in the parking lot.

"Jason, what you did in there was astonishing."

"Yep, it's the last day we're working together, and we've been waiting for a good idea."

"Jason, what I said earlier, I didn't mean it like that, I just waited around for you for a little bit and it took me longer than it should have to realize you weren't interested," Ashley paused and looked down, then looked away. "What was wrong with me?"

"There's nothing wrong with you," Jason said. "It's me. I can't pinpoint it, I don't understand why, but I don't want to have anything real, and you were right there and it was so real."

Ashley didn't know Jason was in a relationship with Megan, but the past several weeks with Brad helped her forget about Jason.

"Well it worked out for me and I don't want this to come between us," Ashley said. "Brad likes you a lot and I told him about what happened with us a few months ago."

The night spent with Ashley had nearly slipped from Jason's mind.

"But we're still friends…and coworkers," Ashley smiled.

She stepped toward him and reached out her right arm for a light embrace. Jason shifted his weight forward and brought his arm up as the two held each other.

She looked up at him as he moved his head down to connect with her eyes as they clutched together. Jason leaned his head forward as Ashley came closer to him.

She opened the back door of her car as they lightly kissed. They dropped into the back seat and Jason reached up to turn off the overhead light.

Afterwards, Jason walked back to his car with his shirt in his hand and pants still unbuckled as Ashley drove away.

He drove back to his apartment thinking of the idea he would present to the task force.

He wasn't concerned about what just happened with Ashley or the possible repercussions. Jason knew Megan wouldn't find out. He also knew Ashley wouldn't tell Brad because she valued what she had with him so much.

So, Jason drove into darkness without a guilty conscience.

15

*A*fter spending the entire morning polishing the presentation they'd pitch to Audi on Monday, Jason returned to his apartment on Saturday afternoon. He collapsed onto the white sheets on his bed and faded into sleep.

When he woke up, the evening sun was already setting. He was frustrated that his entire afternoon had been wasted on sleep. He rose and walked toward the window to look at the sunset.

The sun still had a glimmer of summer left with clouds scattered in the sky.

He read a text from Megan. Her roommates were having a going-away party that night for one of her friends who was moving out of the house.

Jason feared the departing roommate would be Brooklyn Turner. She would disappear from him before he had an opportunity with her. With Megan at the party, he didn't know how to introduce himself to Brooklyn or what he could do to lead into anything further with her. And in that moment, he realized he knew absolutely nothing about Brooklyn Turner, thus his illusion of her was perfect because it was unknown.

He was tempted to scroll through her social media accounts

and search for her like he'd done to so many people before, but he wanted everything to be unscripted and unfamiliar when he first met her. He wanted his mounting interest in her to be entirely objective.

After he showered, he chose a light pink striped button-down shirt. Jason ironed it twice to make sure every wrinkle was removed. He picked his freshest pair of jeans, and instead of wearing his usual pair of shoes, he decided on a pair that had been seldom worn.

Jason looked at himself one final time before leaving his dark apartment.

The party had been going on for a few hours when Jason arrived at the yellow brick house. A group of people circled around the front steps and porch as Jason walked in.

He found Megan in the kitchen with a few friends as music played in the dining room and louder sounds emanating from the basement. The patio door was open; Megan grabbed his hand to lead him outside.

"I was waiting for you, it's been crowded for a while, and I've already had too much to drink."

Jason didn't want to waste time.

"Your text said one of your roommates is moving out, when is she leaving?"

"Tonight's her last night, all of her stuff will be gone by tomorrow. I don't know if you've met Brooklyn yet."

Jason could feel his heart sink when he realized it would be his last opportunity to see Brooklyn. He pried further in hopes that it could spark an introduction.

"No, I don't think I have. Is she still here?"

"I'll go find her," Megan said.

But once Megan entered the house, she was distracted by other people.

Jason knew he'd have a better chance finding Brooklyn without Megan. He walked around the party, but was stopped by several people. The conversations frustrated him. *These people are a waste of time and distractions from Brooklyn*, he thought.

He couldn't find her on the first floor, so he went down to the dimly lit unfinished basement blaring with music. After several minutes spent looking for Brooklyn in the mess of people, Megan pulled Jason and they danced.

He stepped away from her when he noticed an acquaintance. As Jason moved toward him to say hi, he felt Megan grasping at his side and twisting his body leftward.

"Jason, this is my roommate Brooklyn," Megan said.

He turned and his eyes connected with Brooklyn's, freezing him for a split second.

"I'm Brooklyn, nice to meet you."

He didn't have a planned response or scripted greeting. Jason struggled for anything solvent and muttered out a weak response.

"It's certainly nice to meet you as well."

Before he had time to think of a stronger conversation, Brooklyn disappeared into the crowd of people.

Frustrated, Jason followed Megan upstairs to socialize with people in the living room.

Time passed, and the house began to empty. Megan followed a friend who was leaving to the front porch. Jason watched the two talk before getting another drink in the kitchen.

He leaned up against the countertop and sipped on his drink.

"You've been here before, haven't you?"

Jason brought his head up and locked eyes with Brooklyn Turner.

"A few times," Jason replied, at a loss for other words.

"You were here a couple weeks ago standing right there when I came out to get some water. Do you ever leave that spot?" Brooklyn smiled.

Jason was surprised and excited that she remembered the brief encounter. He felt comfortable now. He existed in Brooklyn's world. He started to direct a conversation, but it felt natural talking with Brooklyn. It wasn't forced, it was genuine and mutual. He didn't have to put on a persona; he was fine the way he was.

As the house thinned out, Brooklyn and Jason became the only people left in the kitchen, but that didn't stop the comfortable flow of their conversation.

A young man with short brown hair and a small stature abruptly joined their discussion. Megan became the fourth member of the growing group moments later. It enraged Jason. He felt threatened by the young man he didn't recognize. Jason knew he was more attractive than the stranger, but Brooklyn's attention was being taken away from him.

The conversation continued for a few more minutes until the stranger exited the back door.

Brooklyn turned and shook her head, softly placing her hand on Jason's forearm for a moment. Megan didn't notice.

"He kind of scares me and I've known him since high school."

"Where has Aaron been all night?" Megan asked.

"He's been sick in my bedroom for three hours."

"Aaron is Brooklyn's boyfriend," Megan explained to Jason.

Jason was devastated to hear Megan say it, and was even more annoyed that Megan delivered the news to him. He'd rather have heard it from Brooklyn herself. He had to get over the fact that she was already leaving the yellow brick house, and now in addition, she also had a boyfriend.

It took him a moment to refocus. He couldn't comprehend any sounds. His disappointment was mounting, but he returned to the conversation. When Jason was refocused, he could remember everything him and Brooklyn had talked about. He carefully listened to what Brooklyn shared. Any information could be used for a future conversation.

I don't want to be this way. I want this to be natural. But I need to know everything I can about her while I'm with her. I need to have conversation topics if I see her again.

Megan started cleaning up, which allowed Jason to ask Brooklyn as many questions as possible, picking back up where the two of them had left off before they were interrupted. Jason discovered where Brooklyn worked, her passions and hobbies, how her parents made her mad last week and where she was moving to.

Jason would remember every word of it.

Despite learning that she had a boyfriend of six years, Jason thought the conversation went well with Brooklyn. He appeared to be light-hearted, friendly and sincere. He didn't think he was pretending with her either. He wasn't embodying a character or persona. Being with Brooklyn, Jason simply felt as close to his true self as he possibly could.

Their conversation didn't hit a lull, but eventually, Brooklyn decided to leave it.

"I need to check on Aaron. It was nice meeting you Jason, keep treating Megan well."

She winked at Jason and walked down the long hallway.

Jason's eyes followed her every step until she disappeared from his sight. He feared it would be the last time he'd ever see her. Just as she had walked down the dark hallway and vanished, she would leave his life entirely before he'd more than a few moments with her.

Panic filled Jason's mind as he worried about Brooklyn associating him with Megan. She had to know they were together. He couldn't deny it.

What does Brooklyn think of me dating Megan?

But Jason didn't want to become pessimistic. His conversation with Brooklyn Turner had been the best moment of his week, if not the past few years. He couldn't remember a time when his undivided attention and sole focus had been on another person. Brooklyn had captured all of his attention. He had lost himself in Brooklyn's impenetrable eyes.

She was the girl he could look at and know that there was nothing else in the world he could ever want, that he'd forfeit any and all life pursuits if it meant he could be with her.

Megan socialized with the party stragglers while Jason replayed the conversation with Brooklyn over in his head. Once again, he leaned back on the countertop – which he now thought of as his "place" thanks to Brooklyn – and watched Megan drunkenly talk to those still at the house.

Jason hoped Brooklyn would reappear in the hallway or come to the kitchen for water. He patiently waited, but there was no reunion with Brooklyn Turner. He firmly believed another brief conversation could solidify him as a significant person in her life, so he had every word prepared, but all of it went unsaid.

The final few guests left the house and Megan asked Jason to come upstairs with her. As badly as Jason wanted to tell Megan about his enthrallment with Brooklyn and ask about all her intricacies, Jason couldn't. He walked upstairs with Megan, the thought of Brooklyn Turner completely filling his mind.

Jason laid naked in bed with Megan discussing the party. He hoped she would bring up Brooklyn so he could ask about her. There was no place for him to inquire further, so he quietly listened until Megan eventually fell asleep.

He looked up at the light blue ceiling thinking about his opportunity with Brooklyn. He thought about how if he could have met Brooklyn years earlier, he could have shaped a different path for himself that included her.

Only the uncontrollable future was in front of him, and for that moment, Jason was in a different bed with a different person, just as Brooklyn was in a different bed with a different person.

Jason promised himself it wouldn't be the final time he would see Brooklyn Turner.

16

Before Jason could join the task force for its presentation with Audi, he had to sit through a bi-weekly meeting led by Stanberry. The creative director would push his glasses closer to his face as he flipped through papers, asking about accounts.

The 27th floor conference room was filled with short-tenured associates still learning about the advertising industry. Jason scanned the faces of his dozen peers. Everyone except him seemed to be lost. His coworkers struggled to manage accounts and satisfy their clients while he was working with the firm's best creative minds on a national account proposal.

I don't like to define myself in a corporate standard, but I'm so much better than everyone else in this room. Do they think I'm striving for excellence within the company? I hope not. My mind isn't sedated enough to have a desire to climb the corporate ladder and chase promotions into retirement.

Though everyone in Stanberry's meeting was close to Jason's age, Jason felt out of place. He avoided any social interaction and rarely spoke with his coworkers. With his quiet presence, Jason was believed by the younger associates to be an enigma. Jason enjoyed thinking about their perception of him and did little to change it.

Stanberry started the meeting going over the successes and struggles of the past two weeks. Stanberry rarely changed his tone or inflection until he started recognizing associates for their outstanding work. In his time working for Stanberry, Jason had never been mentioned or recognized.

After brief recognitions, Stanberry asked everyone to briefly update him on the different projects in place. As coworkers updated Stanberry on their current assignments, Jason gazed outside at the rising sun.

He felt his keys and was reminded of a place far from this corporate building that had changed his life.

When Jason was a child, for a week every summer, he would travel with his friend's family to Destin, Florida. Jason's parents never took him on a beach vacation, so the annual trip was his only time to leave Louisville.

As an only child, the beach trip was a reprieve from social obligations and responsibilities that held him hostage at home. He felt free. He'd sit on the beach basking in morning sunlight and watch the sun rise. Before the beach was filled with other vacationers, Jason would watch ocean waves crash into the sand.

When he reached his teenage years, he used the week as an opportunity to write and expand on his deeper thoughts. He'd stand outside on the balcony hundreds of feet above sand and let the cool night ocean breeze wisp around him as he stared at the stars.

The annual trip allowed him to disappear from himself. He didn't have to pretend to be a character or manipulate his interaction with people to gain a good reputation.

He'd spent a week in the same room in a condominium high rise every year for almost two decades. The aging owner from Alpharetta, Georgia had long since stopped bothering with sending and receiving keys to her frequent renters.

Jason knew it was wrong, but he kept the condo key to spark a brief dream of the simple lifestyle it provided. He could disappear. He could write. He could think. He could be free from himself with the key. He thought of it as a failsafe key. If corporate America ever became too unbearable, he could retreat to the condo and beach.

This morning, Jason became so fixated on the key that he imagined abruptly leaving the office to drive to his escape. As Stanberry and coworkers continued to talk, Jason replaced their voices with the sounds of waves crashing into the shore. He pictured his feet digging into the cool morning sand while his mind became entranced with thoughts that only the ocean could pull out of him.

Jason's dream was interrupted when Stanberry called on him to share updates on accounts he was handling. Quickly refocusing, Jason talked for two minutes about the accounts he diligently worked on, lying about all of it due to his lack of preparation for the meeting. Jason hadn't spent much time with his other accounts because of the Audi task force.

Live in the lie.

Stanberry was satisfied with Jason's response and turned to another associate, allowing Jason to return to his daydream.

After the meeting concluded, Stanberry asked Jason to stay longer.

"Don't you have your big Audi presentation today?"

"Yeah, they come in at 11," Jason confirmed.

"Are they going to have you washing the tables or getting people coffee?" Stanberry snickered.

Jason wanted to explain how he'd come up with the signature pitch and would be leading the presentation, but he didn't want to bother talking with someone so inferior to him.

"Yeah, I'll do a little bit of everything; probably take out the trash as well."

Stanberry didn't respond and softly left the conference room.

Jason walked to the window to look at the morning sky before making his trek to the 28th floor.

The six members of the task force gathered in the conference room to practice the presentation. After Jason presented his idea to the group, he had become the leader of the project, deferring only to Downing. Everyone else could now acknowledge Downing's belief in Jason, so the delivery of the presentation was entrusted to the youngest member of the team.

Arthur Howell, Creative Production's head account executive, traveled from Chicago to lend his social skills to the presentation. He met Audi's four executives in the lobby and brought them to the 28th floor.

Downing's team waited in the conference room as they watched the five approach.

Introductions and small talk didn't last long. Downing's booming voice controlled the room as he mentioned the companies and products Creative Productions represented. After trying to prove his agency's worthiness, Downing turned to Jason.

Jason enjoyed public speaking. He liked the undivided attention and chance to display his abilities in front of a captivated audience.

When Jason had time to prepare for a presentation, he considered himself incomparable. He could plan pauses and inflections, pick moments of hesitation and facial expression and use anything to make his audience believe all of it was entirely natural. He had practiced the Audi presentation enough in the last few days to perfect it.

He artistically danced through the presentation, telling the story of Audi's transformation in the hearts and minds of the American public by stating "everything is replaceable." It seemed like a history lesson instead of a pitch.

Jason's monologue could only last so long. He had to turn the four-member audience's attention to Kathy, who would detail the implementation of the advertising campaign.

He never felt nervous when speaking, but Jason was usually on edge more so after he stopped talking in front of a group. He worried about what he possibly did wrong, forgot, and most importantly, what the audience thought of him. He replayed every moment in his mind. As he sat down, he scanned the faces of the four executives of Audi to gauge their interest level.

Downing closed the meeting with his final selling points to remind the Audi executives of Creative Productions' worth.

"Mr. Downing, as you know, we have met with a few agencies already and we plan to meet with a few more. We are impressed with the creative work you produced and we will continue to be in contact with you."

Downing nodded and walked with Arthur Howell outside of the conference with the Audi executives. As Jason watched them walk away, he realized the four executives were faceless to him. He couldn't describe any of the four who had just listened to his presentation.

Four balding white men in black suits and bland ties.

"Now what?" Jason asked his coworkers.

"We wait and hope Arthur Howell knows those boys' favorite lunch spot," Kathy said.

Howell was well-respected and generated a large amount of business opportunities for Creative Productions. After a successful pitch, Howell's relationship with Audi's executives would determine if Creative Productions could land the account.

"When will we hear back?" Jason asked.

"Two days, two weeks, two months, it's all up to them," George Proffitt said. "They aren't in a rush, and we've done everything we can until they decide to get back in touch with us."

Everyone remained in the conference room until Downing

returned. Before Jason could join everyone else's exit for lunch, Downing asked him to stay for another minute. Downing, who remained standing, asked Jason to sit down.

"Jason, you're young and inexperienced, but you were phenomenal today. Your part in the presentation was our strength and the whole pitch came from your idea. I'm impressed with what you're able to do," Downing paused before continuing. "But don't think for a second that we couldn't handle ourselves without you. I've been with this agency for over 30 years. I've seen young hotshots like you come and go, but you know what? They always end up on the streets and I'm sitting here in a corner office making over half-a-million a year."

Downing paused again and looked toward the window.

"Don't make the mistake of thinking we can't do this without you; we've been doing this long before you and this company will continue when you inevitably decide to leave."

Jason's words sounded like they were from Alex Rodriguez's 2015 spring training press conference after his season long suspension from Major League Baseball.

"Sir, I'm part of the team and I just want to contribute."

Downing was impressed by Jason's humble statement, allowing the two to leave the conference room.

Jason rode the elevator and walked into the bustling Louisville lunch crowd.

He knew Creative Productions had a chance to land Audi, but only because of him. Downing wanted to sound powerful, but Jason knew the agency needed him in that moment, and no other creative mind would have done so well.

Jason walked to a food truck for a bagel and water. He found a bench in a small, shaded park. He watched people feverishly moving around city blocks, rushing to the next moment of their lives. Feeling no sense of achievement from the morning's presentation and no viable reason to go back to the office, Jason turned off his phone and watched the active world move forward while he rested on the park bench alone.

I think best when I'm alone. I'm most creative when I'm alone. When I'm around people they're distractions to my best talent. It makes me wonder if I was completely isolated, would I be at my absolute best?

17

I t had been two weeks since Creative Productions had presented to Audi, but no conclusive word had been shared between the two sides. Various rumors circulated around the ad agency including Creative Productions' guarantee for Audi's business while another spread word that Audi would never sign with a Midwestern-based regional firm.

Jason wanted Audi to select his idea, but he didn't care about his company's success. His personal status mattered more. His agency's reputation had no effect on how his social circle perceived him; he had no loyalty to Creative Productions other than receiving a paycheck every other Friday.

He'd watched coworkers celebrate signing accounts, but Jason was indifferent to the business side of his job. The moment he produced a creative idea was also the moment he wanted to create another one. It was a cycle that never ended.

His coworkers reveled in the brilliance of an ad creation, but Jason knew the next day brought the need for a new advertising campaign with a new idea. The factory-like process left him bored and unenthused about the daily chase of ad creation.

Over the next couple of weeks, as Creative Productions

waited on word from Audi, Jason returned to his desk only venturing up to the 28th floor for brief meetings or updates from Downing. Jason's escape from Stanberry had concluded. The tension between the two was higher than ever.

After consecutive monotonous weeks, Jason settled on numbing away his weekend by going to Dexter's Bar on Thursday night with his group of friends and Megan. He ended up at his apartment with Megan.

With Megan alone at his apartment, Jason left for work on Friday morning earlier than usual, potentially to avoid Megan. As he walked to his car with the sun rising in the sky, he worried about what she could discover in his empty apartment.

His friends decided on Dexter's again Friday night. Jason agreed to join, but was disinterested midway through the night because of its resemblance to the previous outing.

Since he slept better alone, he woke Megan up on Saturday morning and told her he needed to go into the office for a few hours. He drove around his apartment complex until she left, allowing him to return to his empty bed exhausted. Two long days followed by two long nights had worn down Jason. He collapsed into his bed.

When he awoke, only a meager pinkish hue dotted the horizon – the beginning of Saturday night. After laying in his bed scrolling through his phone for several minutes, Jason showered and decided to drive to the IHOP on Hurstbourne Lane.

He couldn't remember the last time he'd eaten anything, but he had a burning passion for pancakes, for which IHOP was perfect. He arrived at the sparsely-filled restaurant and sat at a corner booth where an older white woman with unkempt hair waited on him.

"What can I start you out with tonight, honey?"

"I'll take an iced water, please."

Jason was always carefully friendly with all food service workers. He had heard horror stories of cooks and waiters butchering unruly customers' food; he worried about the disintegration of sanitation when he stepped through the doors.

As he waited for his food, he looked around the nearly empty dining area. Even though he preferred to eat alone, Jason couldn't stand seeing someone else dining by themselves. He'd see an older man and wonder about his lonely life, never being able to conform enough to find a significant other. Or a young woman, too dedicated and driven by her career to ever find time for friends. A part of Jason wanted to comfort the lonely people he quietly observed, but he knew there wasn't any way he could help their isolated lives. Yet another part was envious of their content seclusion.

The pancakes were the only food Jason had ingested in the last two days. Alcohol ruined his appetite, so he didn't have any interest eating prior to that night.

After finishing the pancakes, Jason checked his phone to find texts from Keshawn and Megan asking about another night out. He'd spent enough time with his friends in the previous two nights, so he silenced his phone and planned for a night of writing at his apartment.

He left a $10 tip and walked out of the empty restaurant.

Before heading back to his apartment, he stopped at the desolate gas station across the street to fill his empty tank. He stared up at the night sky while his car filled with gas. A purple sedan pulled up to the gas pump beside him.

"Isn't it a little late to be delivering packages?"

Jason turned to the familiar voice.

"Grace, what are you doing here?

"It's a gas station, Jason, a lot of people come here."

The two laughed and another passenger stepped outside of Grace's car.

"Jason, this is my friend Summer," Grace said.

The woman waved to Jason and walked inside.

"Shouldn't you be out partying somewhere tonight," Grace asked.

"I've actually done that a couple nights in a row, I needed a night off."

"Nonsense, you're too young to say that. Come join us, we're having people over at my place. We're a little weird, but it's always a good time."

Jason didn't want to, but the thought of meeting new people always intrigued him. After being around the same group of friends for several years, he wanted to find new perspectives in hopes to challenge his thinking and help him grow.

Jason agreed and followed Grace and Summer back to the house.

When he walked in with the two women, he was greeted by a small crowd of a dozen people. He didn't recognize anyone, but no one asked for an introduction. They acted as if he'd been a part of their friend group for years.

They candidly spoke with him and skipped the small talk on who he even was. He was comfortable around the crowd even though he was five years younger than everyone else there. He and Grace drank tequila from Las Vegas shot glasses with Grace and imitated political figures in front of the amused audience.

Once again, Jason had become the center of attention, yet none of the people around him knew who he was. They had no precognitions about Jason Vaughn, they didn't even know his name.

He walked back to the dining room with Grace to make another mixed drink to sip on.

"I'm glad you came tonight," Grace said. "I'm still not sure how my friends and I formed this group. I'm not even sure if we share anything in common, but I think that's why we always keep getting back together," she said, laughing.

Jason and Grace naturally extended their elevator discussions to talk about corporate life in their shared office building as the night continued. Jason felt fatigued, but he tried to wash it away with another shot of tequila.

The last shot didn't help. He needed a moment to collect himself, so he went to the bathroom and splashed water on his face. He looked at himself in the mirror with his eyes drooping and bags circling around them.

Do you ever look at yourself in the mirror and get surprised by the person you're looking at? I do. I know that can't be me, or maybe it is. Sometimes I don't know.

When he walked out of the bathroom, Grace approached him.

"Jason, the band of motley misfits has a new guest for you to meet."

Grace gently tugged Jason by the arm and brought him back into the living room. Jason hadn't completely turned into the room when Grace started talking again.

"This is my cousin Brooklyn, you two are the young ones, so don't make the rest of us feel old. Brooklyn, this is Jason, we work in the same building."

The girl who had violently erupted into Jason's life and then disappeared had returned. He hadn't forgotten about her in the past two weeks even though he'd doubted he'd ever see her again.

Brooklyn and Jason looked upon each other and laughed simultaneously. Jason kept his eyes directly connected with Brooklyn's stare.

"We've met before, at a party at my old house," Brooklyn said.

Surprised by their previous encounter, Grace concluded the introduction, which was the first one that night.

"Well if you two already know each other, you're ruining the fun for the rest of us that want to remain anonymous."

Grace joined the people sitting in the living room as Jason followed Brooklyn into the dining room.

"So, you work with Grace?" Brooklyn asked.

"We work in the same building. We see each other in the elevator sometimes. She randomly saw me at a gas station and invited me to this," Jason answered.

Brooklyn smiled, "What are the odds of that. I don't even know how she managed to drag me over here tonight. I actually had a few other things I was invited to."

"Well I'm glad you chose to come," Jason said.

They continued to talk in the dining room.

"Where's Megan tonight? I assumed she'd be with you," Brooklyn asked. "You're still together, right?"

Jason wanted to answer "no" to prove to Brooklyn his freedom and commitment to pursuing her, even though he knew she had a boyfriend.

"Yeah, but I wasn't planning on doing anything tonight until I saw Grace, so I didn't get a chance to invite Megan."

Jason didn't want to be able to predict what Brooklyn would say, but he knew what was next, even if he hoped for the opposite.

"Aaron couldn't come tonight. I don't think you two met at the party. He's been so busy working on the house, he went to sleep hours ago."

Jason didn't allow his disappointment to alter his focus as the conversation continued.

Without any disruptions, the two stood next to each other while everyone else remained gathered in the living room. Jason couldn't remember the last time he had been so dedicatedly interested in a learning about someone else's life. Brooklyn rarely looked away as if to demand Jason's entire focus on her. He felt her presence paralyzing him. The entire night was starting to feel like a dream, and he didn't want to wake up.

Flawless people were rare; you might meet one or two in a lifetime. Brooklyn Turner was one example of perfection embodied in a human that Jason would encounter in his life. He watched Brooklyn's mouth move and her facial expressions contort as he comprehended everything she said. Her smile had a comforting aura that was begging to be captured, in film, in memory. But nothing would do it justice.

The night had stretched past two when Brooklyn decided to leave.

"I should be getting back. I don't want Aaron to worry where I am; I told him I would only drop in to see Grace."

Jason agreed with Brooklyn's idea and walked to the front door while she talked to Grace.

As the two walked out together, Grace waved to Jason. He thanked her for the invitation. Jason imagined other scenarios when Brooklyn and he could leave a party together, walking down the stairs as a couple.

Brooklyn looked up at the night sky when the two reached their cars, parked right beside each other.

"It was nice talking to you tonight. It was different, in a good way," Brooklyn paused. "Grace seems to meet everybody. You'll have to check on her for me during those elevator rides."

Jason knew the coincidence of seeing Brooklyn couldn't be replicated again without the intrusion of Aaron or Megan.

"I don't want this to sound weird," Jason started.

"When people start with that, it usually is," Brooklyn interrupted.

"I don't talk to people as well as I do with you," Jason said, sliding his foot across the pavement. "I'd like to be able to see you again. Do you think we could exchange numbers?"

Brooklyn smiled before dropping her head and running her hand through her hair.

"I had a great time tonight, but I'm in love with a man I have been with for the past six years and you're dating my former roommate," Brooklyn hesitated. "I don't think anything good would come from that."

Jason's body decompressed in disappointment.

"I guess we're too attractive for our own good," Jason joked.

The two laughed together and embraced each other with their eyes while standing ten feet apart.

"It's endless," Brooklyn said, looking up.

"What?," he said, confused.

"The night sky and the stars. It makes us seem so small."

Jason shrugged and nodded his head.

"Goodnight, Brooklyn."

She smiled and got into her car.

Jason thought of her as he drove back to his apartment. Similar to two weeks ago, he didn't know when or if he'd ever see her again.

He had promised himself two weeks ago that it wouldn't be the last time he'd see Brooklyn Turner. Tonight had only reaffirmed that guarantee.

When he returned to his apartment, he parked and laid on the windshield of his car. He looked up at the starry night sky, knowing Brooklyn Turner was looking toward the same endlessness giving him enough comfort to fall asleep.

18

alf of the next Monday lulled by and Jason was drifting to sleep at his desk when his phone sharply rang. It was Downing's administrative assistant requesting Jason come to the 28th floor conference room immediately.

Even though he thought the other members of the task force would rush to Downing's demand, Jason casually made his way to the floor above. After two weeks, Jason had no sense of urgency.

After arriving on the floor and seeing the conference room, Jason knew the meeting's agenda.

Victory filled Downing's face as Jason walked into the room. Downing tried to hide his excitement and secret, but even the most oblivious could notice his brimming smile of satisfaction.

"You might've already guessed, and it's well-earned," Downing said joyfully. "We officially landed Audi. We just signed them."

No one could contain their excitement except Jason. He nodded his head and shared in handshakes, but didn't feel any more accomplished than he did when he was dozing off at his desk 20 minutes ago. Downing quieted the group and began to outline details and expectations for the management of the account.

"Audi's executives are going to meet us at our main office in Chicago for preliminary objectives," Downing said.

Kathy asked Downing if everyone would travel to Chicago for the introductory meeting.

"No, it will be only two of us," Downing firmly said. "Since Jason did such a nice job on the initial ad creation and pitch, he'll be going with me."

"Are you sure you want him to go with you? He is just a kid," Michael Davies said.

George Proffitt was obviously frustrated with Downing's faith in Jason.

"My office is right next to where we'll meet them," Proffitt said. "If they're coming to my city, it should be me representing us."

Downing coldly stared at Proffitt.

"No George, you'll stay here and continue to work with the team," Downing said. "Jason and I will be leading this one. It's not a debate, it's been decided."

Jason liked Chicago and anything to get away from the office was good. He was pleasantly surprised by Downing's selection. With the trip scheduled in several weeks, Jason hoped for crisp autumn air to replace the stagnant September sun.

With seemingly the entire task force voicing their frustration to Downing, Jason knew there would be no celebratory drinks or words of congratulations.

It was well before five, but Jason had already had enough of the workday, deciding to leave earlier than usual. He thought Stanberry had already left, but as Jason walked toward the elevator, Stanberry rushed to catch him.

"I heard you landed Audi," Stanberry said in an oddly excited tone.

Jason didn't want to give Stanberry's acknowledgement any satisfaction.

"Without doubters there wouldn't be any miracles," Jason said.

The elevator door opened, and Jason stepped in. After descending a few flights below the 27th floor, Jason stopped the elevator and reversed it. He pressed the button for the 33rd floor.

He wasn't sure if Grace would still be working, but he entered the Great American Insurance office. Surprised by the unfamiliar face, the receptionist quickly questioned Jason's intentions.

"Can I help you?"

"Yes, I'm looking for Grace's office."

I don't know Grace's last name.

"Grace who? Do you know her last name?"

"Just tell her that Jason Vaughn is here to see her."

The skeptical receptionist made a call, seemed disappointed by what she was told on the other line, and got up to lead Jason further into the office.

"Follow me."

Most of the offices and cubicles were empty, but the entire

floor seemed fresher and more exciting to Jason than his six floors down.

"Jason, you picked the right time to come, I just scammed some senile elderly folks into giving me money for fake life insurance," Grace joked. "And now you're visiting me, and my day is made."

Jason laughed as the perturbed receptionist closed the door.

"What brings you up this high today?"

"I had some spare time, I wanted thank you for inviting me to your party," Jason softly said.

"Everyone said you were fun to be around," Grace said.

As Jason opened his mouth to comment on her hosting skills, an interrupting phone call abruptly cut him off.

"Thanks for coming up, you should stop by more often," Grace said as Jason stood up to leave.

"Oh, and Jason. She couldn't stop talking about you the next day. She was very impressed."

Jason may have rationalized seeing Grace so he could thank her for the invitation, but his true intention was to learn more about Brooklyn. The receptionist was gone from the front desk when Jason left. He felt a bit of achievement in Grace's final words, much more than signing Audi earlier in the day.

Jason wondered if Grace would tell Brooklyn he stopped by. He wondered if he could confide his pursuit of Brooklyn Turner with Grace. He wondered if Grace would aid him in his pursuit of her cousin, or if she would defend Brooklyn's relationship with the consistently-absent Aaron.

Jason pondered these questions as he walked to his car several blocks away.

After disregarding Megan on Saturday and Sunday, Jason felt obligated to take her to dinner on Monday night. She arrived at his apartment just past seven. The two traveled to downtown Louisville to a Mediterranean restaurant on Fifth Street.

"So, what did you do Saturday night? Everyone was asking about you."

Jason knew he had to hide the truth.

Live in the lie.

"I was so tired. I just stayed at the apartment," Jason said. "I fell asleep so early, it was a boring night."

No worse from the unknown falsehood, Megan continued talking cluelessly.

After the dinner, Megan lingered at Jason's apartment for an hour before leaving for the night. Jason escorted her outside and watched her drive off. Thankful she had left, Jason sat in silence in his empty apartment until drifting off to sleep with thoughts of Brooklyn racing in his head.

19

On Friday night, Jason's friends went bar hopping in downtown Louisville. Jason wanted a social night away from Megan, so he didn't invite her, but that didn't keep her away. He caught sight of her talking to Heather and Naomi when he walked into Julie's house. Jason didn't like how Megan had seamlessly fit into Jason's friend group, that she was invited to their get-togethers without his permission. He wondered if he'd be replaced by her when they inevitably broke up.

Jason tried to avoid her while everyone else mingled around Julie's house, but her curiosity and unconditional attraction to him forced her to approach him.

"Why didn't you tell me about this?"

"You already knew about it, so looks like I didn't need to."

"Yeah, Julie invited me last night. Everyone's been asking where you've been lately."

You were invited before even I was?

Keshawn broke the tension between Jason and Megan by asking where they wanted to go first. It was past midnight when the eight friends climbed into two cars and headed downtown.

During the 15-minute car ride, Megan held Jason's hand and playfully flirted with him in the backseat. He didn't want Kyle and Julie to see her affection, so he pushed away Megan's hand and told her to stop several times.

Jason liked watching the bars' younger crowd. He remembered his younger days when the Louisville bar scene was new to him. He fed off the energy of the city's lights without any thought of growing older. In his mid-20s, Jason was at a unique age where he could still be comfortable in bars filled with college-aged patrons while also fitting in with older crowds at smaller spots.

Before walking into Barillas, their first bar of the night, Julie stopped Jason as the rest of them filed in.

"You've got to get it together. You're being so standoffish with Megan. Why aren't you being nice to her. It's like you don't even like her."

"What are you talking about?"

"Megan has been so sweet to you and you're being a dick," Julie answered. "Do you even want to be with her?"

Live in the lie.

"Of course I do," Jason lied.

"Well act like it, at least be nice to her," Julie said. "God, Jason."

Relationships. Just one big distraction from actually doing really good. How many people were prevented from doing great things because of focusing their attention on their interpersonal relationships? I'm sure a person started doing a study on that, but got interrupted by a dinner date.

"Okay, you're right."

My friends won't stop pressuring me with Megan. Then they wonder why I don't bring girls around. They just can't stand to see me mistreat her. It isn't mistreatment, it's lack of attention. I won't devote all my time to making sure she is okay. They are always telling me how I should be better to her.

Jason didn't know many people inside the bar, so he was able to spend more time with Megan. He bought her several drinks and took her out on the dance floor. It was past 1 a.m. when Jason went to the bar to get another drink as Megan stood with their friends. From across the crowded bar, Jason noticed Brooklyn Turner standing around a huddle of people.

With a drink in hand, Jason paused for a moment hoping to make eye contact with her. She didn't divert her eyes from the conversation with the people around her.

Jason didn't recognize anyone that stood near her, but he assumed the man standing next to her was Aaron, her boyfriend. She continued to talk with her friends, so Jason returned to his group in need of a strategy to talk to Brooklyn.

After some awkward banter, Jason convinced Keshawn and Kyle to move to an area closer to Brooklyn. Julie and Megan followed. Even though Megan lived with Brooklyn, Jason wanted the interaction with her to be without their significant others.

Megan drifted away to talk to Naomi and Heather several minutes later. Brooklyn noticed Megan as Jason watched from afar as the four talked for several minutes.

As soon as Brooklyn stepped away from the three, Aaron

rejoined her for another drink at the bar. Jason examined the couple and wondered if Brooklyn knew he was there.

Jason stood near Megan in hopes that she would make her way to Brooklyn eventually. He wanted to sneak into a conversation with Brooklyn to remain a thought in her mind. However, surrounded by a circle of friends and Aaron, there was no viable way for Jason to get Brooklyn's attention.

He saw no outwardly intense connection between Brooklyn and Aaron. He didn't think Aaron completely appreciated Brooklyn's vibrant immaculateness, perhaps because he'd become so accustomed to it. Jason would never have allowed her perfection to casually exist without it entirely consuming him.

Aaron walked to the bar to get another drink, allowing Jason the chance to follow him. He compared himself to Aaron in the mirror. Aaron had straight dark brown hair and thick eyebrows with pale skin. His eyes were small, but soft and forgiving.

We're both the same height, I might be a little taller. I have a stronger frame. I'm more attractive than him and my hair is nicer. He is dressed fine, but I'm dressed better. How can someone so average be with Brooklyn Turner?

Jason looked at Aaron who had everything Jason wanted as he waited for his drink. The two went separate ways as Jason returned to Megan, who opened her arms as he approached, while Aaron rejoined a tightly protected Brooklyn. Jason kept an eye on Brooklyn in search of an opportunity to greet her.

It was near 2 a.m. when Brooklyn left her group of friends

in the far corner and walked to the bar alone. Jason strayed from Keshawn and moved close enough to Brooklyn for her to see him.

He'd been looking at her all night, but as soon as he got the chance to speak to her, he didn't really know what to say.

"I thought you went star gazing on Saturday nights."

Brooklyn looked up and smiled.

"The planetarium doesn't close until four, it's not too late," she said.

Brooklyn winked at Jason, turning away and walking back toward her friends.

Jason's first attempt at a conversation had been wasted, but Brooklyn returned for another drink 20 minutes later. Jason followed her again, in hopes of initiating a longer conversation.

"Funny how you only need a drink when I come up to get one," Brooklyn said.

"Funny how you only come here when you know I'll see you," Jason answered.

Brooklyn softly smiled as she raised her right eyebrow, "And you don't worry my boyfriend's going to notice you're meeting me up here every time?"

"I don't think he is noticing you at all."

"Why have you been staring at me all night?" Brooklyn asked, a more serious look on her face.

Jason wanted to tell Brooklyn that she was the only thing worth looking at, that her beauty was worth his full and undivided attention, but before he said anything, Aaron joined the two.

"Is this one of your work friends?" Aaron asked as he approached Brooklyn at the bar.

Brooklyn brought her arm around Aaron as she introduced Jason.

"Aaron this is Jason, Jason this is Aaron, my boyfriend. We went to high school together."

"Oh cool, nice meeting you," Aaron said with a disinterested handshake, already leaving the two and heading to the restroom. He kissed Brooklyn on the cheek. "I'll be back in a minute, babe."

With Aaron gone for a few minutes, Jason talked freely with Brooklyn until Megan interrupted their conversation. Brooklyn became focused on catching up with Megan and ignored Jason's attempt at flirting with her, so he returned to Keshawn and Julie.

"That girl Megan is talking to is something else," Keshawn said.

Since Jason considered Keshawn and Julie his closest friends, he thought about sharing his dream of Brooklyn Turner with them. He didn't know how Julie would react, so he didn't say anything.

"She *is* beautiful," Julie said. "I think she's Megan's old roommate."

Julie continued, "Keshawn, you should go over there and say something to her."

Keshawn and Heather had been quietly together for two months, which Jason and Naomi knew, but Julie was still unaware. Keshawn didn't answer Julie as Naomi and Heather made their way to join them. The five sipped their drinks for a few minutes until Jason and Naomi separated from the group to take a breather at the bar.

Jason caught Brooklyn looking at him as he walked toward the bar, which caused a devious smile.

"Now, how do you plan to convince her to give you change?" Naomi asked.

"Get who?" Jason responded.

"Brooklyn…I think the whole bar has noticed the two of you looking at each other the whole night and going up to get drinks at the same time. You know she's in a serious relationship?"

"She's been looking at me?" Jason smiled.

"Your real problem is how you're going to get rid of Megan," Naomi ignored Jason's question. "I know you won't break up with her and she isn't smart enough to know you're cheating on her."

Live in the lie.

"I'm only focused on Megan," Jason said. "There isn't another girl I'm pursuing."

"Stop that." Naomi demanded.

"Stop what?" Jason asked.

"You can't do that with me, I know you too well," Naomi said.

The two returned to their friends as the crowd started to thin.

It was past 3 a.m. when Brooklyn and her group gathered together to leave. As she started to walk toward the door with her friends in front of her, Jason noticed Brooklyn left her phone on the table she was standing near. He picked up the phone and started to follow her outside.

As he walked outside with the phone, he gladly found she had no passcode and he hastily typed in his name and number into her contacts.

When he made it outside, he saw her standing across the street.

"Brooklyn…you left your phone," Jason said as casually as possible.

She turned and looked into her small wallet. She walked toward Jason relieved.

"Oh, thanks, I completely forgot it was on the table," Brooklyn said.

Brooklyn thanked him again and began to walk away. Before she got too far, Jason asked a final question.

"Why did you tell him you knew me in high school? Why not that we met a few weeks ago?"

"I don't know, I guess… I just thought it sounded better? We were talking for too long for you to be some random acquaintance."

"I'm a random acquaintance at this point?" Jason asked.

Her group of friends a few hundred feet in front her called out, "Brook, c'mon, let's go."

With every ounce of strength in his body, Jason used unscripted words as his heart pounded through his chest.

"Because you make me feel so helpless," Jason said.

Brooklyn, who had already started to turn away, stopped.

"What?"

"You asked me why I kept staring at you tonight. It's because I feel so small around you."

"Now Jason," Brooklyn paused, smirking. "Let's not compare me to the stars in the sky; I don't want people thinking I'm that old."

Brooklyn winked at Jason and left to catch up with her friends. She slightly turned her head back twice as she walked away.

Jason leaned back on the building across the street from the bar. Through the window of the bar, he watched Megan happily dance around; Keshawn and Heather talked to each other in a nearby corner. Julie, Naomi, Kyle and Brandon were circled around a table.

His friends were content with their lives, but Jason couldn't begin to grasp the thing he wanted most.

He debated whether he should rejoin his friends inside the bar, but he realized their lives would continue to move forward as he observed from a distance, regardless of his interaction.

His group of friends finally walked outside and called Jason over.

"Where were you? We were looking for you," Julie said.

The eight friends staggered back to their cars parked a few blocks away with Jason behind them.

Without anyone in coherent distance of hearing, Naomi slowed down and turned to Jason.

"If she's the girl you really want, you wouldn't want her

to leave her boyfriend in a split second, but you'll get a chance with her, you always do," Naomi said.

"No, this girl is going to be different," Jason responded.

"I can't remember the last time you didn't say that about the next girl you were chasing."

"Just wait," Jason said.

"I'm not going to wait at all. I'm out on this one. You're on your own. You need to break this off with Megan before it goes too far. She's in so deep already and you don't even realize it or even care."

Jason was frustrated more than usual with Naomi, so he didn't respond and walked to the car alone. As he drove back to his apartment from Julie's house with Megan asleep in the passenger seat, he rolled down the window and let the cool night air free his mind of any thoughts except the music playing.

20

I t was a rainy Thursday morning when Brooklyn and Aaron nearly arose in unison to prepare for work. They each had separate routines, but walked out of their house together a little before 8 a.m.

The two kissed each other and parted ways, the harmonious "I love you" resounding in their ears as the cars started and drove off in different directions.

Brooklyn turned on her windshield wipers and thought about her day ahead. She didn't have any sales calls, conferences, conventions or trips scheduled, so she could spend the entire day at her office.

When she settled into her desk, Brooklyn looked out the window at the grey clouds and rain.

Her coworker Hannah walked into Brooklyn's office a little past 10 a.m. to discuss their weekends.

"Are you all moved in with Aaron now?"

"Yep, these past two weeks are the most we've ever been around each other," Brooklyn said.

"But everything's transitioning smoothly?"

"We're seeing new sides of each other. It's been great. He still has a few things to learn, but so do I," Brooklyn answered.

"How much longer is he going to hold out on you?"

"Aaron isn't holding out on me," Brooklyn said. "Neither of us want to rush into marriage before we're ready."

"Too soon?! You've been together six years. I've been waiting for a bridal shower invitation from you for the past three."

Brooklyn and Hannah continued to talk until 10:30 a.m., when Brooklyn went down the hall to her sales manager's office for a meeting. She had worked under Jerome Felton for the past three years, developing a strong relationship with him.

Felton was well-respected around the region. Brooklyn went to him for professional advice and sales tactics. Though Brooklyn was close with her father, Felton and she had a relationship comparable to a father and daughter, but this was vested together by business.

There were meetings and events where he would be the only African American while she was the only female, the commonality of those shared experiences brought them together.

On Thursday, the two sat across each other as they reviewed the current week and prospects. He manicured his words in order to motivate and challenge her, always asking more from her. After talking for 30 minutes, the meeting concluded, and Brooklyn stood up to leave.

"One more thing Brooklyn…the convention you went to in Atlanta, did you meet Richard Vance there?" Felton asked.

"I did on the first day, but he left early," Brooklyn said. "Do you need something from him?"

"I lost all his contact information. Can you send it to me?" Felton said.

"I have it on my phone, I'll send it right now," Brooklyn said.

She scrolled through a lengthy contact list to the V's.

After moving past a few names, Brooklyn stopped in surprise by the name on the screen.

The name 'Jason Vaughn' was listed just below Richard Vance.

Stuck in a temporary lapse, Felton reawakened Brooklyn. "Did you find it?"

Halted by her momentary surprise, Brooklyn refocused and sent the contact information to Felton before leaving his office.

She first remembered the night Jason asked for her number. She then thought of Saturday night when the two saw each other. Brooklyn was positive there was never a point when she typed in his number. After thinking about her encounters with Jason, she decided it must be a prospect or client who shared the same name. She searched through the company's customer management database, but found no one named Jason Vaughn.

Her heart raced as the screen became frozen with his name and number listed on it. She fell into temptation and tapped 'send message.' His phone number turned blue and she was connected to iMessage.

Brooklyn blankly looked at the screen for a few minutes wondering what she should type or if she should send anything at all. Her intent focus on her phone broke when a coworker asked her to go out for lunch.

She agreed to join, but put her phone inside the desk drawer when she left. Midway through the meal, Brooklyn decided she would delete the phone number to prevent anything from happening.

Aaron wouldn't want her texting a guy she'd met a few times in random social settings, she thought. She wouldn't tell Aaron about the phone number because nothing good could come from it, nor did she remember how the number was in her phone to begin with. Could she have been too drunk to remember? But she clearly remembered when Jason handed her phone to her so she couldn't have been that far gone on Saturday.

When Brooklyn returned from lunch, she looked at the contact information for Jason Vaughn, but couldn't bring herself to deleting the number. She decided his phone number could stay in case she needed to talk to Megan or use his advertising connections.

She couldn't stop her interest and intrigue as the afternoon continued. She decided to text the number in the solitude of her home before Aaron got home. She predicted Jason would make another pass at her, which she would once again remind him that she was happily in a committed relationship that had spanned for six years.

Brooklyn felt nervously self-conscious about texting Jason. She hadn't texted anyone in this way for years.

The final few hours of the day passed by as Brooklyn's

anxiety continued to build from the thought of sending a text to Jason Vaughn.

When she returned home, she took off her clothes and changed into a tight white V-neck and shorts. Barefoot, Brooklyn lay on the couch in the living room and once again looked at the name that brought her so much intrigue.

Just as she tapped the text message box, Aaron pulled into the driveway. In a bout of fear of infidelity, Brooklyn rushed to put her phone in desk cabinet.

Misguided for a moment, Brooklyn returned to her life with Aaron by greeting him at the door. He was happy to see her after a long day. The two went about their evening routine. They ate dinner together around 8 p.m., discussing their day's nuances and occurrences. After they finished, Aaron flipped on the television while Brooklyn read a novel she started a week earlier.

Aaron had to wake up earlier than usual the next day, so he showered and went to sleep early, leaving Brooklyn with her book.

Lured in by an empty living room, Brooklyn pulled her phone out of the desk cabinet and scrolled through the emails and messages she had missed. She responded before leaving her phone on the kitchen counter.

Aaron was already asleep when Brooklyn decided it was late enough for her as well.

She walked out to the kitchen to drink a glass of water under the night skies. Deviating from her usual routine, Brooklyn brought her phone outside.

Looking at Jason's number, her heart began to race as she typed out a message. The night breeze helped to cool her as she felt her body become hot when she pressed send.

Brooklyn stared up at the night sky and read over in her mind the message she had just sent.

'Is this Jason'

She hoped he wouldn't text back, or even better, a wrong number. A few minutes passed and she was nearly certain it had been a coincidence that one of her old contacts shared the same name as the Jason Vaughn she knew.

And then, three dots appeared across her screen. Whoever was on the other end of the message was typing back.

'yes, who is this?'

She was satisfied to get a response, but was hesitant to text back.

'Brooklyn Turner. How did I get your number'

'i gave it to you?'

'When'

'at the bar saturday.'

It made sense to Brooklyn now. She had left her phone on the table, Jason picked it up, and before returning it to her, typed in his number.

'You typed it in before you gave me back my phone'

'yep.'

Brooklyn was infuriated that Jason had violated her privacy by using her phone. She didn't plan to send another text, but Jason sent another message.

'i did it for your own safety. you don't know anyone else who can fight someone with an umbrella.'

Jason's text ignited enough curiosity in Brooklyn that it sparked a conversation as the two rapidly sent messages back and forth for a few minutes. Finally, it had become too late for Brooklyn to continue texting, so she ended the conversation.

'Say hello to Grace tomorrow I'll see you'

'hey have a fabulous night.'

Brooklyn looked up at the stars one more time and walked into the bedroom where Aaron slept.

"You were looking out there for a long time. Did you see anything special?" Aaron quietly asked.

"Sorry, I didn't mean to wake you."

She laid next to him and the two embraced for a few minutes before Aaron drifted off to sleep. As Brooklyn was clutched in Aaron's arms, she thought about Jason Vaughn.

She wondered why she had an intensified urge to text him. Though he was wrong for putting his number in her phone, she did send the first text. She wondered what Aaron would think if he found out that she had been texting Jason while she was outside. She wondered if she should say anything to her friends about Jason. She wondered if she should delete the messages on her phone from him.

And most importantly, she wondered what Jason thought of their conversation that night and when it would happen again.

21

The crisp autumn air filled Jason's lungs when he walked out of his apartment to meet Downing for their trip to Chicago.

A black Audi A-6 pulled up to the curb. With the engine still running, Downing stepped out of the driver's seat door.

"Put your bag in the trunk. Don't wreck the car until after we meet with them."

Jason obliged and took control of the new car.

It was still early in the morning, so Jason didn't want to talk on the drive. He muttered responses softly in hopes that Downing would eventually drift to sleep during the drive. Downing was slouched in the passenger's seat sleeping by the time they passed Seymour, Indiana. Jason was tempted to turn on music while driving across the flat lands of the Midwest, but feared it would annoy Downing.

They arrived in Chicago a little before noon. Downing booked two rooms at the Swissotel near Millennium Park. It was the nicest hotel Jason had stayed in. After checking into the hotel, Downing and Jason went to Creative Productions' main office to work through their final thoughts before their meeting with Audi the next day.

Creative Productions' Chicago office was several blocks off Michigan Avenue in a tall, nondescript black building.

"If you keep working, I could see you being a big name here one day," Downing told Jason as they walked into the building's lobby.

Jason dismissed the comment because of his disinterest in moving up the corporate ladder at Creative Productions.

He liked the size of Chicago, but it couldn't compare to the pace of New York City. Jason had been to both cities several times. He liked the overwhelming size that Manhattan provided. If Jason wanted to climb a corporate ladder, he wanted it to be in New York.

Downing and Jason toured the expansive three-floor office space before working on their final preparations.

When the fleeting fall sun dipped beneath the other buildings, Downing announced enough work had been done for the day. The two walked back to the hotel to return to their rooms, agreeing to go to dinner later that night with Downing at an Italian restaurant a few blocks away.

"Jason, you drove here," Downing said. "Get whatever you want, this one is on the company."

He wouldn't have agreed to dinner with Downing if they were paying separately.

"Thank you, I'll pick the next one up," Jason said with a smile.

After the two finished dinner, they returned to the hotel. Like a father would tell a young child, Downing gave Jason instructions for the remainder of the night.

"You're free for the night, but remember, we need to be at the office by 10 a.m. I wouldn't do anything too much tonight if I were you; you'll have plenty of time to explore the city later."

It was still early, but Jason took Downing's advice. He flipped through television stations while he rested on the bed. He couldn't remember the last time he watched television.

When Megan called around 9:30 p.m., Jason was indifferent as he listened to her talk about the day. He searched for a brief pause in the conversation and wondered which excuse would successfully allow him to hang up without irritating Megan.

An audio recorder would do the same thing I do on phone calls with her.

A week earlier, Megan ended a night they shared together by saying "I love you."

Jason was sickened by hearing it. He said "thank you" until she forced him to say it as well. He didn't want to hear "I love you" and having to say it disgusted him even more. Megan was forcing him to say it at the end of every conversation.

'I love you' should go unspoken. How I am supposed to know what love is? I don't feel it; do other people? Or are they just pretending because they watched or read something that makes them think it exists?

What if emotions aren't real? We're programmed since birth by our parents, friends and people around us about these feelings. But where do they come from? Did we accept emotions as real during ancient times as a reason to fight against the human crisis of life? Was the idea of love created in a cave because it rationalized and distracted us from being hungry and cold? Once the idea of emotions was created, we were infected.*

Megan would always say it first, but required Jason to follow, not leaving his apartment or car until he did. Jason was determined to end the conversation this night, so he blurted it out and hung up.

After he placed his phone on the nightstand, he thought of the simplicity of relationships before love became a factor. Every part of a relationship seemed to be simple, but once "love" entered it, everything seemed to mean a lot more than it should have.

Before he went to sleep, Jason looked out the window at the city lights and active streets below. He looked at the distant stars before he closed the curtains; they were much harder to see with significant lights covering the sky, preventing Jason from seeing the constellations he often saw from Louisville.

Downing knocked on his door the next morning at 9:30 a.m. The two walked to Creative Productions' office and waited for Audi's executives to arrive.

The three executives from Audi spent several hours reviewing with Downing and Jason what they wanted Creative Productions to address and manage. One of the executives initially mistook Jason for Downing's assistant, but that error was quickly corrected by Audi's two other representatives that had already witnessed Jason's abilities.

The five worked through lunch in the conference room and concluded the meeting in the late afternoon. Audi's executives were pleased with the direction Creative Productions had planned. The three told Downing and Jason they were returning to their corporate headquarters in Virginia the next morning.

Downing made evening plans with an old friend, so Jason was alone for the night. He handed the keys to Downing, who drove off once they returned to the hotel. Jason walked around Chicago for a few hours. He passed the Tribune Tower and felt the bricks, stones and rocks from famous places around the world.

Eventually he checked his phone: two missed calls and three unread texts from Megan. He turned his phone off and walked under the city lights. The people walking on the chilly October night energized Jason to explore more of the city.

He walked to the desolate Navy Pier as the cold wind from Lake Michigan whipped against his body. Jason reached the edge of the pier and turned to gaze upon the entire city of Chicago. All of it stood in front of him as he rested by himself under the night sky. An entire city moved before him as he quietly observed from afar.

Jason couldn't take any more of the icy wind, so he went back to the hotel. Instead of returning to his room, he stopped at the relatively empty hotel bar. He sat down at the far end and the bartender approached him a few minutes later.

"What'll it be?"

"Whiskey sour."

Jason studied the other patrons as he sipped on his drink. After drinking a few more, Jason was ready to leave, but an older man with tousled white hair sat down next to him, delaying his departure.

"They're sharing a drink called loneliness, but it's better than drinking alone."

Jason chuckled, "Billy Joel?"

"That's right…I come here every night, drink two drinks and walk home," the older man said in a thick Midwestern accent.

"Every night?" Jason asked.

"Well, see, in hotels, the people I meet tonight are gone tomorrow. I meet a new person every day and never see them again. No hellos, goodbyes, just a casual conversation and we each move along with our lives."

"What happens if I come back tomorrow night?" Jason said.

"I'll be too drunk to remember you."

Jason laughed; he liked the older man's ideology.

"People are afraid to be honest about themselves because they fear it'll change how others see them," the older man said. "But with me, these people say what they want, and I won't hold it against them. You'd be surprised what people will tell a complete stranger."

Jason decided to stay for another drink and keep the old man company, but also out of curiosity. He wanted to hear more of man's philosophies. Jason's tab continued to grow, but he didn't care.

"Before you leave, answer me one question, why are *you* here tonight?"

"I don't know," Jason said.

"What brought you here, business?"

"Yeah, my boss and I are meeting with a client," Jason answered.

"Well that takes the fun out of it; I was thinking your lady left you."

Jason shook his head, "No, just a business trip."

"You have a lady back home?" the older man asked.

"Yeah," Jason paused for a moment. "But I don't treat her very well. She's good to me, but for some reason, it just doesn't click for me. I want to feel something, but I can't."

The old man asked, "What do you love?"

Jason thought for a moment.

"If you have to think about it, then you don't love anything yet, but you will soon," the older man said before Jason could answer.

"So, I should be searching for 'the one'" Jason said.

"How did I know my wife was the right person for me?" the older man paused. "Because I never questioned it."

"You should be teaching relationship classes," Jason joked.

"Why don't you find yourself someone new? Chicago's a big city. There ought to be one out there right enough for you."

"I've always been looking for the right one, but there's always too much missing for me to fully value the people," Jason said. "I don't think finding someone significant is for me."

"I used to be just like you. I thought I was a bad man unworthy of anything special, but you'll find someone that makes you feel like you did all the bad things just to get to them."

"That's what you call love?" Jason asked.

"No, that's what I call an expensive escort."

Jason burst out laughing and the old man slapped him on the back.

"Go on home. It's time for me to walk back myself."

With his head spinning, Jason closed out his tab and calmly made his way to his floor, stumbling down the hallway to his room.

Jason turned out the lights and fell into the bed. He turned on his phone and flipped through Megan's text messages, but didn't respond. He didn't listen to her voicemail.

After texting with Brooklyn Turner one night several weeks ago, Jason scrolled back to reread the conversation. As he reached the bottom of the texts, he began typing a new message.

He realized he was too intoxicated to send anything, but he looked at the three dots that stayed on his screen that signified she was typing. He looked at the dots and wondered what to type.

After a few minutes, he started to drift into sleep as he looked at the screen. His eyes were jolted open when three dots appeared on the opposite side of the message thread. Brooklyn was typing.

The three dots from Brooklyn's typing and the three dots from Jason's typing stayed on the screen as he intently watched. After a little more than a minute, the dots from Brooklyn's side of the thread disappeared. Jason's screen went blank.

He fell asleep on the white hotel sheets with his head still spinning.

22

"I need your help."

"What's going on?"

"You know I shouldn't be going up and down stairs anymore."

"Are you hurt?"

"No, and I'll be fine...I'm supposed to be at a meeting at 10 a.m., just signatures, it'll be quick, can you help me?"

Naomi knew she'd be helping Clarence before she even answered his call.

"Send me the files and I'll take care of it."

Naomi found a suitable folder for the paperwork and walked to a building several blocks away from her office. She flipped through the pages as she walked across the pavement in the morning sunlight, just like she watched her mother do years ago.

Clarence's client, a small bookstore owner on Frankfort Avenue, had the front portion of their store destroyed by a drunk driver, who crashed into the building last winter. The driver, Andrew Watkins, had been killed in the single-car collision.

Clarence and the Watkins' family lawyer had come to a

settlement, where a portion of Watkins' life insurance policy would be transferred to the bookstore to cover the damages. Naomi's mind was put at ease when she realized no lawyers would be present at the meeting. She only needed a signature from Watkins' insurance agent for the forfeiture of assets in his policy.

She walked into the Great American Insurance offices on the 33rd floor.

"You don't look like a Clarence Kline," a woman in her early 30s said as Naomi opened the conference room door.

"I'm not," Naomi said as she walked into the conference room. "I'm Naomi, his paralegal."

"Hi, I'm Grace."

The two sat across from each other at a wide table surrounded by empty chairs. After the initial introduction, Naomi and Grace quietly organized the documents before them.

Naomi turned through the paperwork, marking where signatures were necessary. Her mother taught her to be efficient during meetings that involved paperwork to prevent any chances of second thoughts to occur. Naomi knew that wouldn't happen this morning, but she remained curt.

"Twenty percent of Mr. Watkins' policy is forfeited to the bookstore for the damages incurred following the wreck by Mr. Watkins last January. The amount can be transferred to the account listed. We already have signatures from our end, so I just need your signature as Mr. Watkins' insurance agent."

"All right, I can send over our completed forms to you as well," Grace said.

"That's not necessary, we have everything from Mr. Watkins' estate already," Naomi said.

Naomi looked at Grace, who was fidgeting with a pen on the other side of the table as she looked through the paperwork. Naomi could tell Grace was uncomfortable, but it wasn't because of Naomi's aloofness.

Naomi stared at Grace, whose head remained tilted downward.

"Did you know him?" Naomi spoke aloud.

"What."

Grace didn't know how to respond. She looked at Naomi from across the table, then at the paperwork, then back at Naomi. Silence filled the conference room; the steady stream of air from the vents in the ceiling was the only respite from the stillness.

Naomi wanted to press further.

"Considering his family's wealth and your inability to look at me when I say his name, I'd think Andrew Watkins—"

"We were engaged," Grace interrupted, and then paused. "At one point. We were together for almost seven years."

"Did he start drinking before or after you split," Naomi gently asked.

Grace combed her right hand through her hair, sighing.

"Before. He started to spiral out of control after his first DUI. I tried to stay with him to support him, but I just couldn't, I wasn't strong enough."

"How long ago was it?"

"A few years ago. I kept control of his insurance, he didn't care. I don't think he imagined going through a building."

Grace hadn't cried since Andrew's death, but knew she was on the verge of tears in front of someone she hadn't even met before, a complete stranger.

"You wanted to help him, but didn't know how," Naomi said softly.

The two women looked directly at each other from across the table.

Grace felt as if the young woman looking at her could feel everything she'd experienced. The love her and Andrew shared for each other when they were young, the process of their maturity together, and then, the eventual corrosion and split, ending in a strictly professional relationship that had lasted for the past several years.

The two stayed silent for a moment, looking into each other's eyes from across the table.

"Want to know a secret?" Naomi paused without allowing the question to be answered. "I'm not a paralegal for Clarence Kline. He isn't competent enough to be a practicing attorney, but he needs the money, so I secretly do work for him. If anyone found out, he'd be disbarred, his cases tossed out and I'd probably face a hefty fine, if not jail time."

Grace looked taken back as she wiped a trickle of tears away from her eyes.

"Why'd you tell me that?"

"Sometimes it's easier to tell things to complete strangers than to the people we know."

The two passed paperwork back and forth in the conference room for several minutes without saying another word. Naomi gathered her files and prepared to leave. Grace stood up in unison and escorted her to the elevator.

The elevator stopped and Naomi got in, but before the doors closed, Grace looked to Naomi.

"How were you able to do that?" she asked. "Make me feel a little less alone?"

"You just have to be willing to notice people," Naomi answered.

"That's a gift," Grace said.

As she rode the elevator, Naomi realized this was the building Jason Vaughn worked in. She couldn't remember the advertising agency's name, but she smirked thinking of what persona Jason would be putting on for his co-workers today.

The elevators doors opened, and she walked outside of the building. She was no longer a paralegal or lawyer. She walked back to her own office and her own job, not once thinking of her mother or what she could have become.

Naomi was her own woman, and that's all she wanted to be.

When she returned to her desk, she became immersed in her work. Before she realized the rest of the office was empty, it was well beyond 7 p.m. She called Brandon to say she'd be home soon. She walked through the empty office, scanning co-workers' desks and cubicles on her way out.

Before returning to her car in a nearby parking garage, she walked to a small city park and found an open bench. The wind breezed through the trees waiting for the days until its leaves would fall. The cool air chilled her as it whipped around her, yet she was warm inside. Everything was right.

She was alone, but she felt loved. The people she needed most were no longer with her, but she felt as if they were beside her. They'd given her life and would continue to do so.

As she sat entirely and observably alone on the park bench facing city streets, she felt connected to her world. She knew no one would ever need to rely on her, as she would never need to rely on others, but she also realized that everyone had helped her, as she'd helped them, too.

Darkness filled the night, but the battle of light and dark was being won, not by the lights that sporadically lined the sidewalks and streets, but instead, by the light of her soul. She was alive and she could feel it, never so in the way that others may feel alive, but in a unique way she could only express with herself.

The breeze continued to build, but the dropping temperature couldn't force her off the park bench, that though she may forever be searching, but she would never be alone.

23

*A*fter returning from Chicago, Jason returned to his desk and regular assignments while sporadically venturing to the 28th floor. October had given way to a colder November and so had Downing's usage of Jason increased.

Jason hadn't fallen out of a favor, but Downing knew Jason's greatest ability was used in the initial idea's creation. Jason had performed well and didn't want to be more involved than necessary. He liked the decreased workload, which gave him more time to daydream or walk around the office. He was relieved when Downing said his daily trips to the 28th floor conference room would become more infrequent.

Without the distraction of Audi, Jason fell under the constant tutelage of Stanberry once again. The time away from his boss had made his dislike of Stanberry worse.

After changing the water cooler, which Jason did every ten days in the 27th floor break room, he looked outside to the bustling streets below.

"There you are," Stanberry abruptly announced. "I need you to see a client for me at 11."

Stanberry's inferiority complex is at an all-time high. He knows

I went to Chicago with Downing. He knows I'm untouchable now. Anything he says to me is an empty threat. To have no respect or power over someone you supervise must be awful.

"Are they tired of seeing you?" Jason answered.

"No," Stanberry said as he allowed a brief smile to cross his face. "It's an old friend, Rich. He wants a little consulting work done. He wants to keep it in-house for his practice. He's a doctor."

"Okay, you said 11?"

"Yes, he's in St. Matthews, I emailed you the address and information."

"I didn't know you knew how to use email," Jason said.

Stanberry shook his head.

"He's a good friend of mine. Do whatever you can to help him out."

Jason nodded and left the break room.

Anything to get away from the office for a little bit.

Jason spent 20 minutes reading over information on Rich's practice before leaving. He arrived a few minutes before 11 a.m. The walls were stale gray and chairs bordered the waiting room. Several patients tilted their heads as Jason opened the door from the main lobby.

Rich met Jason at the receptionist's desk.

"I'm Rich. Don't bother calling me a doctor, I hear it all day," A man that had recently passed middle age said to Jason. "I thought Chuck was going to make it out himself, but he said you're as good as it gets. I told him there was no way you could be as good as him, but he said you were the best. What's your name?"

"Jason Vaughn," Jason said to the doctor whose glasses firmly held just in front of his eyes. "I can't promise I'm as good as Mr. Stanberry said I was, but I'll see what I can do for you."

"If you're learning anything from him, you'll be great."

This guy can't actually believe Stanberry is good. And why is Stanberry saying good things about me? That must be a lie.

Rich showed Jason around the practice while discussing his challenges in growing his practice. The two sat in his office and Jason went through ideas for Rich to promote his practice.

With so much mind-numbing work over the past few weeks, Jason became actively involved in the consultation. He didn't use any pre-catered jargon to overwhelm Rich. Jason wrote out the ideas and marketing strategies. After the meeting had extended beyond an hour, Rich was satisfied with Jason's help.

"No wonder Chuck speaks so highly of you. Thank you so much," the doctor said rising from his chair. "I'll see you out the door. I actually have another meeting at noon."

Jason exited the waiting room into the building's first-floor lobby.

He brought his head up in time to see Brooklyn Turner walking toward him.

The two made eye contact from across the lobby and converged in the center.

Brooklyn tried to hide a smile as she spoke first.

"What are you doing here?"

"My pediatrician keeps telling me 25 is too old but I keep coming anyways," Jason joked.

Brooklyn raised her right eyebrow to demand an answer.

"I had a meeting with Dr. Vance," Jason paused. "Why are you here?"

"What a coincidence, I'm here for Dr. Vance too," Brooklyn said. "And I'm running late, it's nice to see you."

Jason said goodbye and watched as Brooklyn walked into Rich's office.

He was overcome with a rush of excitement as he walked back to his car. He started his car and idled in the parking spot for a few minutes. Instead of driving back to the office for another monotonous afternoon, Jason turned off the engine and stood outside his car.

He waited for 27 minutes, but finally, Brooklyn walked outside of the building. Her heels lightly tapped the pavement as her hips contoured to her high-waisted pencil skirt. Her hair was tossed to one side because of the fall breeze that cooled the air.

Brooklyn peered at Jason with confusion and anticipation as he began to talk.

"I had to make a few phone calls, so I stepped out for some air before going back to the office."

"Right," Brooklyn said slightly annoyed. "Because you have to hold your breath once you get in your car."

"Do you have time for lunch?" Jason asked bluntly.

"What? No...Jason, I can't," Brooklyn responded. "We're in St. Matthews, people know us. They can't see us together."

"They'd probably think you were meeting a client for a business lunch, and if people know me, they'll think the same thing."

"I don't know, Jason," Brooklyn said. "I don't think so."

"I'll make you a deal. We will sit at separate tables and I'll whisper just faint enough for you to hear me," Jason offered.

"Why don't you just tap out Morse code?"

Jason laughed and told Brooklyn to follow him in her car.

Though his driving skills were impeccable, Jason's car was not.

He had saved money to purchase a used car in high school and hadn't bothered with replacing it. He usually wasn't embarrassed by it, but the 15-year old car didn't match Brooklyn's sleek black sedan. She didn't mention anything about it, though, and before long they parked at a café.

The two sat across from each other in a public setting for the first time. Brooklyn kept her eyes diverted toward the menu for the first few minutes. After they ordered, the two eased into a conversation.

"It's not a coincidence we saw each other today," Jason said.

"You believe in fate?" Brooklyn asked.

"No, it just happened. I don't make the mistake of confusing coincidence or fate for absolute randomness," Jason said.

"So you're not a man of science and you're not a man of faith, what are you a man of?" Brooklyn said.

Jason was stumbled by the question. His brow became wrinkled as he thought of an answer.

"I am a man of nothing. We live and then we die, and there isn't anything significant in between."

Brooklyn shook her head, "If you really believed that, you wouldn't have asked me to lunch today. You wouldn't have sat in your car and waited until I walked out."

Jason didn't have a response, so he shifted the conversation to lighter topics. The two continued to talk while leisurely finishing their meals. Jason watched as Brooklyn ate.

She uses her utensils as a model would in commercials. She chews so softly and stays so quiet. I can't think of a time when she isn't absolutely gorgeous.

When the waitress brought out one check, Brooklyn became flush.

"Can you split that, we should have said it earlier," Brooklyn awkwardly asked the waitress.

"No, it's okay," Jason intervened. "It's not that much. I'll use my company card and tell my boss Rich wanted to go out to eat."

She doesn't need to know I don't have a company credit card. I'd rather have her leave guilt-free than thinking she owes me a few dollars. That has to be the only lie I ever tell her.

After the credit card was returned, Jason followed Brooklyn to their cars to part ways.

"Jason, I want to ask you something," Brooklyn said as she opened her car door.

"Of course, sure."

"What do you want from me?" she said.

"What?"

"You've met me a few times, whether it's coincidental, fate or science, I don't know, but you know Aaron and I know Megan," Brooklyn paused. "What are you trying to get out of this? You know this can't go on any further."

Jason couldn't quote from a movie or book; instead, he tried his best to find the right words. He didn't have a lie to tell.

"There's going to come a day, and it might not be tomorrow or next week or next month, but there will come a day when you want to see the world differently, live your life in a way that you never thought you could," Jason said. "And when that day comes, you'll know I'm the person that can do that for you."

Brooklyn sighed and flipped her right hand through her hair.

"Jason, I don't doubt who you are and that you have a special way about you, but I found the person I'm going to spend the rest of my life with already. You'll find that one day too."

"I don't want anyone but you," Jason answered.

"You don't even know me," Brooklyn softly muttered.

"I promise you, I will," Jason said.

"Jason, I can't see you anymore," Brooklyn said firmly.

"I know," Jason said defeatedly. "So, what now?"

"We get into our cars and drive off to our separate lives," Brooklyn said.

Jason smiled and nodded before watching Brooklyn get into her car and drive away. After her car disappeared in the distance, Jason silently sat in his passenger seat for a few minutes. Jason had started to believe fate had brought Brooklyn and him together, his trust in this destiny had never been stronger.

He had a plan to get Brooklyn Turner.

24

ason could hear friends' voices filling Julie's house Friday night as he opened the front door. He greeted Megan with an unusually authentic smile. Jason didn't internally mock or mimic Megan as she replayed the events of her day, sipping on a beer.

He asked questions and intently listened. She continued to talk until Keshawn intervened.

"We're ready to go," Keshawn told Jason. "Can you drive?"

The eight friends shared two cars on the trip to Circle's. The anticipation of alcohol eased Jason's system as they walked through the front door.

Jason and Keshawn recognized several familiar faces and broke off from the group in their usual routine.

"You guys must live here," a short brunette said as she hugged Jason and Keshawn before rushing to another person.

"Do we know her?" Keshawn laughed.

"I recognized her, but I don't know her name," Jason said.

Jason noticed that Keshawn's eyes never drifted far from Heather, who huddled around their other friends in a crowded corner.

"We can go back to them," Jason said after catching Keshawn glance at Heather again.

"No, let's keep going around," Keshawn said in attempt to hide what Jason already knew.

They moved around for several more minutes in the crowded lower area before Keshawn directed Jason to a table.

"I want to tell you something. For the past couple months Heather and I have been together," Keshawn said to Jason. "We didn't know how you guys would react, so we kept it quiet."

Jason smiled, "You've done a poor job hiding it."

"What...who else knows?"

"No one," Jason answer. "Just Naomi and me. I found out at the lake."

"Were we that obvious?" Keshawn said.

"No, but I just know you," Jason said, smirking. "Naomi knew before me."

"She's always been more perceptive than you," Keshawn joked.

"I beat her sometimes," Jason said.

"You two haven't said anything to anyone else, right?" Keshawn asked.

"No," Jason paused. "It's your news to share. It's not my business to get into it."

"I wanted you know more than anyone else."

"Well let's get back," Jason said, pointing to the crowd filling the bar.

They returned to the table with Heather, Megan and Julie.

"Kyle's in the bathroom, Naomi and Brandon are getting another drink," Julie announced when Jason and Keshawn arrived at the table.

I like watching Heather and Keshawn interact. I can see their happiness. Their secret makes it even better to witness.

Megan led Jason onto the dance floor a little past 1 a.m. Jason brushed against her slender body as the two lost track of time. After a while of dancing, Megan pulled Jason away from the dance floor and asked if they could stop at her friend's house on their way home.

Jason said goodbye to Naomi and Brandon, who were talking to a group of people Jason didn't recognize. Megan waved to other friends before staggering out of the front door.

With his ears still ringing from the music and his senses dulled from alcohol, Jason listened to Megan's directions as he drove. The house was close to Jason's childhood home, so he coasted down the typically busy roads without drifting into other lanes.

Some of the stale green lights began to turn yellow and red. Jason was close enough to the neighborhood and it was late enough in the night that he began to drive through red lights when no other cars were nearby.

Megan continued to talk about her friend as they approached the neighborhood several hundred feet away.

In an instant, red and blue lights flashed on in the rearview mirror.

The feeling of sobriety flushed into Jason's system.

"Hold on."

Jason revved up the engine and took a sharp left turn into the neighborhood with the flashing lights following.

"Jason, what are you doing?" Megan screamed.

"This is it for me, I can't get pulled over. I'll lose everything."

"Jason, pull over." Megan demanded.

Jason had driven these neighborhood roads since he had his license. He had walked and biked through area since he was a child. He knew every street, bump and tight corner.

Sober or not, this cop can't keep up with me on these roads.

He weaved in and out of subdivisions, finally finding a driveway to slip into, quickly turning off the engine and lights. The neighborhood was silent.

"Jason, he hasn't been behind us since we turned into the first subdivision," Megan said, exasperated.

"Do you think he got my license plate?" Jason firmly asked.

"I don't think he was going after us," Megan said.

Jason was relieved. He started to quietly laugh. Megan uncomfortably joined him as they drove slowly to her friend's house. Megan introduced Jason to her three friends before socializing. Jason sat in a chair away from the three and waited for Megan to ask to leave.

"Can I stay at your place tonight?" Megan asked when she was ready to go an hour later.

Jason drove back to his apartment. He carried Megan into his bedroom after she stumbled out of the car. After Megan fell asleep, Jason left his bedroom. And his apartment. He walked to his car and drove away from his apartment. Jason continued to drive into darkness until he pulled into a driveway of a small house in Hikes Point.

Dried leaves crunched beneath his feet as he walked across the front yard. He reached the door and softly knocked three times. The still fall air whisked through the emptying trees as Jason waited at the doorstep. Footsteps tapped against the hardwood floor and the door clicked open.

"Jason, what are you doing here?"

Naomi stood at the door for a moment, and then walked outside, closing the door behind her.

"I want Brooklyn Turner, but I don't know how to get her."

Beyond acknowledging his pursuit of Brooklyn to her, Jason hadn't shared his intentions for her to anyone.

Naomi grabbed Jason's arm and moved him several steps from the door.

"Brandon is right inside, if he hears you…why'd you come this late?"

"I need to know what to do," Jason said.

With weary eyes and a tired body, Naomi accepted the beginning of the conversation with a sigh.

"Why do you want her so badly?" Naomi asked.

"She's perfect. She's the girl I've been waiting for all this time."

"And is she the answer to all your problems?" Naomi said.

"She will be," Jason stated.

"Sometimes we think people are the answers to our problems, but they never truly are," Naomi paused. "Our solutions don't come from other people, they come from us."

Naomi didn't let Jason respond.

"You only want her because you don't have her. You want the beginning of it, but you don't want anything that comes after that," Naomi said. "Your only focus is getting her, once you do, you don't know what to do after that happens."

Jason shook his head, "I can tell; she's going to be the girl I can change everything for. I can be the person I want to be with her."

A car drove by the house. Naomi and Jason didn't speak until it went further down the street.

"Jason, you're so desperate to share the intricacies of your life with anyone," Naomi said. "But you wouldn't know what to say even if you found the right person."

Jason sat down on the steps in front of the house.

"I keep asking 'Who am I?' but I should really be saying 'Who I am.'" Jason said.

"I think you know who you are, but you keep searching for why you are the way that you are," Naomi said. "She isn't going to be able to help you with that answer."

"I know she will," Jason said.

"Let's say you guys get together," Naomi said, sighing again. "What happens in five years, when you're out with her one day and you see someone younger, more vibrant and more beautiful than her, won't you be drawn to that person?"

Naomi stepped down to sit next to Jason.

"The settling stillness of contentment is too much for you to bear," she said. "The utter perfection of a simple life is too beautiful and unscathed for you to accept, ordinary is too precious for you."

"You think I'll be unhappy for the rest of my life?" Jason asked.

"Yes, Jason, I do," Naomi said. "Because I don't think you want to be happy."

"Why not?"

"Because you fight with yourself every day," Naomi said. "You aren't who you want to be, but you don't know how to change. The answers you keep searching for aren't ever going to come."

Jason put his hands on the back of his neck, "What went so wrong? Why am I like this?"

"I don't know," Naomi whispered. "But one day, I hope you find it."

"Find what?" Jason asked.

"Freedom from yourself," Naomi said.

She stood up and walked toward the door. Jason heard the door close and lock turn. He sat on the steps silently as the cold fall air rushed into his lungs.

25

Instead of pressing the 27th floor button on Monday morning, Jason altered his usual routine. The elevator doors opened on the 33rd floor and Jason made his way to the familiar receptionist for Great American Insurance without a backstory in mind.

"Is Grace in yet?"

He was told to wait in the reception area until she arrived. He sat down and watched for the elevator doors to open. Grace appeared a little after 8:30 a.m.

"You must really need me if you're coming here on a Monday morning before nine," Grace said after opening the glass door.

"You're not going to believe how many social security numbers I got this weekend," Jason said as he followed Grace to her office. With a raised eyebrow, the receptionist stayed silent as the two walked back into the office.

Jason closed Grace's office door and sat down at the chair across from her desk.

"I need help with Brooklyn," he said. "I want a chance with her."

"Did you become senile overnight?"

"I'm being serious," Jason said.

"So is every other guy that has ever met her, but she's marrying Aaron so you should stay away from that long list of ill-suited bachelors," Grace said.

"I want one date," Jason said. "Can you get that for me?"

"Of course I can," Grace said with a mocking laugh. "Now do you want a table of three with Aaron sitting with you or were you thinking he could chaperone from afar?"

"You're the only way I can make this happen," Jason pleaded. "I need you."

Grace slightly turned away from Jason to look out her office window.

"Brooklyn and I grew up together," Grace said staring outside. "I was always the older cousin that everyone wanted to be friends with in order to be a friend with Brooklyn. She was the pretty one everyone had to meet. I was just the person that brought them to her."

She turned back toward Jason, whose eyes were fixated on the carpet.

He stood up and started to walk to the door.

"I want to be able to show you something," Grace said before Jason opened the door.

He turned back around, "What?"

"I'll do it," Grace said. "I'll set up your night with Brooklyn, but there's something you need to see, that I'll show you."

Jason agreed and intently listened as Grace planned his opportunity.

Grace would find a night Aaron was away on business and

invite Brooklyn for an evening out. They would plan to meet somewhere, but Jason would be there instead of Grace. It was simple enough, so Jason left pleased with the agreement.

Two weeks later, Jason returned to Grace's office with the night set. Aaron was away from Louisville for a few days, so Grace asked Brooklyn to join her for dinner. She agreed to a place downtown, allowing Jason to find his ideal venue.

Jason spent three days planning the Wednesday night dinner with Brooklyn Turner. He listed conversation topics on scrap paper, trying to predict awkward moments and plant transitions to keep everything flowing smoothly. He hadn't spent this much uninterrupted time with Brooklyn, so he worried that she'd walk away from him at any moment during the night.

He shopped at several department stores for new clothes despite having plenty of choices already in his closet. He decided upon a pair of fresh dress shoes he purchased in the fall. After a full day of anxiety and fidgeting around the office, Jason got ready at his apartment for a night where he hoped he could convince Brooklyn to give him a chance.

It was a relatively cold night in mid-December as Jason stood outside a small restaurant on Main Street where Grace had said they would meet. After a few minutes passed, Jason began to worry Brooklyn had uncovered their scheme.

Ten minutes later, Jason nearly convinced himself to leave, but Brooklyn appeared on the opposite side of the street. The wind twisted her hair as she walked toward Jason in a slender black peacoat. Jason watched her walk elegantly across the street in clean black heels.

Brooklyn made eye contact with Jason several hundred feet away, locking her eyes directly onto him. She didn't smile or say anything until she came within a few steps of him.

"Why did I have a feeling I wouldn't be spending time with Grace tonight?" Brooklyn asked plainly.

"You could have turned around at any step before this one," Jason smiled. "C'mon, I have a table for us just down the street."

Brooklyn hesitated at first, but eventually followed Jason, her intrigue growing with every click of the pavement.

He had reserved a table for two at Linzio's, one of the most exclusive restaurants in Louisville. Some tables were reserved months in advance while walk-ins were rarely accommodated. Jason had done work at Creative Productions for Linzio's, the owner and his restaurant for several years, so a personal phone call was enough to get a reservation.

Jason and Brooklyn walked into the dining area filled with the city's elite class. They were out of place, but they were young and beautiful, two undeniable qualities that the deep-pocketed patrons couldn't buy.

Linzio, whose well-kept white hair and small stature demanded admiration as he walked through the dining area, visited Jason and Brooklyn's table soon after they arrived.

"Mr. Vaughn, I have to thank you for the entire crowd that you've provided me tonight and every night," Linzio said with a cheery smile.

"People don't need billboards to want to come here," Jason laughed lightly.

"Now who is this beautiful young lady you're with tonight?" Linzio said.

"Oh, forgive me, this is Brooklyn," Jason said.

Linzio nodded and smiled, "What wine would you two want for dinner? I'll send out our finest."

This night has started as well as I could have hoped.

"First you collude with my cousin to meet me again and then you take me to the best Italian restaurant in the city," Brooklyn said.

"Are you impressed yet?" Jason said.

"You're doing what every other guy does, you're just doing it in a nicer restaurant," Brooklyn said as she tried to bite away her smile.

"But I'm not finished yet," Jason said.

Brooklyn sipped on wine while Jason looked into her eyes without any apprehension of reprisal. After a long dining experience, the two said goodbye to Linzio and left. A few flakes of snow fell from the sky as Jason and Brooklyn walked down Main Street.

"There isn't anything better than walking with a beautiful girl under the city lights," Jason said.

"What if it was two beautiful girls?" Brooklyn joked.

"One is enough for me," Jason said.

He led Brooklyn further down Main Street to a small local art gallery.

"Have you seen the new exhibit?"

Brooklyn affirmed Jason's assumption and said no.

"Let's go take a look."

Brooklyn followed as Jason walked up a set of stairs on the side of the building leading to a set of double doors. The building's security guard came forward several minutes later and unlocked the doors.

"I thought you were coming 30 minutes ago," he said.

"How long do we have?" Jason asked.

"Let's say 45 minutes," the security guard said.

For nearly an hour, Jason and Brooklyn moved up and down the three-story gallery with brick walls viewing impressionistic artwork from around the country. Brooklyn paused at every painting, allowing Jason to watch her visual analysis of the artwork.

"How did you get us in here?" Brooklyn asked as they walked back down the stairwell after their allotted time was over.

"My friend has worked here for years," Jason said. "I thought you'd be able to appreciate the artwork more with it empty."

Jason handed the security guard several $20 bills as he escorted them out of the building. When the two returned to the city streets, a light snow had accumulated on the ground as it continued to fall from the sky. Jason deviated from his script, calling for a horse and carriage that was strolling around the block.

The black carriage had four covered candles at each corner and was pulled by a brown horse. As the carriage slowly made its way around downtown, the soft snow fell on their faces. Brooklyn and Jason's conversation had gone quiet for a few minutes, but the comforting silence was aided by the repetitive clack of the horse's hooves.

It was rare that Jason ever felt completely comfortable, but as he ran his hand through his hair and looked at Brooklyn, he felt content.

I'd do anything to avoid aimless physical contact, but I'm going to hold her hand.

Jason softly placed his hand on top of Brooklyn's right hand. She didn't look down, but didn't move her hand either.

What if I never have to let go?

Jason ended the carriage ride when it reached a coffee shop on Third Street.

Though Jason didn't drink coffee, he shared a cinnamon roll with Brooklyn as she drank a small latte. Midway through a discussion on the best movies no one has ever seen, Brad and Ashley, two of Jason's co-workers from Business Week, approached to Jason's table.

"Jason Vaughn in a coffee shop, seems abnormal to me," Brad said as he shook Jason's hand.

"I didn't know you knew how to talk to girls," Ashley said, stopping to look at Brooklyn.

"This is Brooklyn," Jason said.

They talked for several minutes, but his two co-workers left when their order was called.

"I've introduced you to three people tonight," Jason said. "You should bring your business card next time."

"Who said anything about there being a next time," Brooklyn said.

The two smiled sadly as the severe reality of their other relationships filled their minds. They finished a conversation before leaving the coffee shop. With more than four hours gone by, the two walked back to their original meeting place.

"Where'd you park?" Jason asked.

"I'm just past that light," Brooklyn said, pointing a block down the street.

And though the night had started well and transitioned eloquently, neither of the two knew how it should end.

"Jason, I can't remember a night like this ever," Brooklyn paused. "But I don't know what happens next. I don't know where we go from here."

"I'll give you a kiss goodnight and we'll both walk away from each other knowing this won't be the last night we share together like this," Jason answered.

Brooklyn scoffed, "Aaron will be back, I can't be going around like this."

"You may love him, but you're hopelessly captivated by me," Jason said.

"When do you think that wears off?" Brooklyn said.

"I want to find out," Jason said.

Jason lightly clutched Brooklyn's waist and pulled her closer as he slowly leaned down. Their cold lips met for a moment as Jason could taste the peppermint in Brooklyn's mouth.

Whether it was the night air or something else, Jason felt chills flow through his body as he pulled Brooklyn closer.

It seems perfect. The first time for anything is always the best. I have to live in this moment.

The two were forced to break away and without any words being spoken, Brooklyn slowly walked back to her car. Under the streetlights and falling snow, Jason watched her leave.

For the first time, Jason realized he was no longer on the daunting pursuit of Brooklyn Turner. He finally had her. He walked back to his car smiling, awaiting the future that stood ahead, but for the night, he would drive off knowing he gave Brooklyn Turner the perfect night.

26

When Aaron's car pulled in the driveway late Thursday evening, Brooklyn felt guilt from the previous night. She had been so consumed with thoughts of her date with Jason that the consequences of her decision had evaded her for the time being. She hadn't returned to the reality of her relationship with Aaron until he arrived at the house.

Brooklyn had never considered anyone other than Aaron before, so he never questioned her loyalty. Before he reached the door, she checked her phone a final time to make sure any evidence of Jason Vaughn had been deleted. She tried to pretend like the previous night never occurred when the door opened.

She had trusted Aaron with so much of her life over the past six years, so she feared an admission of guilt could ruin their relationship. She wanted to tell him the truth, but needed to find the right moment. She could be honest in saying that Grace had planned the evening with her, but things were altered. She could skip the elegant dinner, art gallery tour, carriage ride and kiss, all of which could risk the relationship.

The two greeted each other and within the first minute,

Aaron asked about the previous night with Grace. The responsibility to be honest drilled into her chest.

"It was nice," Brooklyn said. "She brought a new guy she's interested in; she ended up getting sick pretty early on, so I spent most of the time with him."

"That's very nice of you to stick with him," Aaron said genuinely. "Why don't we all go out one night together? We haven't been out with another couple in a while. Who is it?"

Brooklyn held back deliverance of the truth after being stumbled by the question. She swallowed deliberately, "Jason Vaughn, they met a few months ago."

"It's about time she found someone," Aaron said. "We'll get something planned for us after New Year's. I know just the place."

Brooklyn was frightened by the thought of a double date with Aaron and Jason. After Aaron left the room, she frantically started to text Grace about the upcoming issue, but before she could send it, he walked back into the room and she deleted the message.

Later that night, Brooklyn lay in bed with guilt and lies fuming from her as Aaron slept unaware of the unconsecrated secrets.

When Jason woke up Friday morning, he could feel his body still brimming with confidence from Wednesday night. He didn't talk to Grace Thursday about his date with Brooklyn, so he headed to the 33rd floor when he arrived Friday morning.

He walked toward the receptionist's desk at Great American

Insurance after exiting the elevator, but the receptionist blocked him before he could go any further.

"Grace won't be in this morning," he said sternly.

"Do you know what time she'll be back?" Jason asked.

"This afternoon, but she'll be catching up on work, so I doubt she'll time for unwelcomed visitors," the receptionist said.

Staring into the wrinkle-surrounded eyes of the older man, Jason stepped closer to his desk.

"What's your problem with me?" Jason said.

"It's men like you that ruin everything," he said. "I can see vacant eyes."

"You don't even know me," Jason said.

"You're careless," the receptionist paused. "You have no regard for anyone around you and you never will."

Jason had enough and returned to the elevator without saying anything else. Downing was waiting for Jason when he arrived at his desk.

"You're meeting with Paul at 10 a.m. upstairs," Downing said.

The CEO of Creative Productions, Paul Harbaugh, was visiting the Louisville branch today.

"Who else will be there?" Jason asked.

"Just you," Downing answered.

Shaking hands and running through introductions is a big enough chore, but to sit down with a CEO for an hour is going to be unbearable.

Jason opened the bottom drawer of his desk and pulled

out three ties. He walked to the restroom to select the best tie. Stanberry trailed Jason to the restroom to ask him about the meeting with Paul.

He follows me like a whipped puppy. He'll be begging for information when the meeting's over.

Jason assured Stanberry he would learn as much as possible before slapping him on the shoulder to dismiss his superior.

By quarter to 10, Jason couldn't wait any longer. He decided to venture to the 28th floor conference room.

In a $10,000 suit, Paul Harbaugh sat alone in the corner with a firm posture. His thinning white hair and well-groomed beard looked immaculate. His glasses rested below his eyes and didn't seem necessary other than being an added accessory. Without hesitation, Jason walked in.

"And you must be Jason Vaughn," Harbaugh said from across the room.

The CEO stood up and shook hands with Jason. Introductions didn't last long as Harbaugh began to ask Jason more serious questions. He kept a notepad next to him.

This is like a job interview.

"When can you come to Chicago permanently?" Harbaugh asked. "We need your talent up there."

Jason paused and thought. "I can't see myself living in Chicago," Jason answered.

Harbaugh scoffed and shook his head.

"It's our headquarters," he said. "Imagine the big accounts you could handle. Think of the doors we could open together.

And a promotion like that, money wouldn't be an issue anymore."

Think about the first person that invented a door. Was he trying to keep people in or out?

Jason dismissed the comment, "What about New York City, why haven't you expanded there?"

Harbaugh avoided Jason's question, "You can't be a creative account associate for the rest of your life. There's too much on the table for you to pass this by."

"I don't really care," Jason said.

Harbaugh was confused by Jason's indifference. He spent his life climbing the corporate ladder and rising to become the CEO of Creative Productions. He was driven by the desire for achievement in corporate America, so he couldn't comprehend why Jason would turn any of it away.

"Why?" Harbaugh asked.

"None of it matters to me," Jason said. "All of you desperately struggle for ideas, designs and creations that take me a few minutes to do. I can live without this, but you can't survive without me."

"We bring in nine-figures of revenue every year and we continue to grow. You haven't done anything for us, son," Harbaugh said, laughing lowly.

"You're growing because of me, Audi's the biggest account this company's ever had," Jason said.

"What do you want then?" Harbaugh said. "Money doesn't seem to matter, recognition doesn't either. What are you searching for?"

"Mr. Harbaugh, I'll do my job, and I'll always be indifferent about it, so you're going to have to live with that because you need me," Jason said.

"And you don't think for one second I could fire you and not miss a beat?" Harbaugh said.

"Everything is replaceable," Jason smirked.

Harbaugh burst into laughter.

"Damn it, you're good," he said. "I can't figure you out, but I want you on my side."

Jason left the conference room with a mystified CEO still in it.

After a long lunch with Keshawn at a downtown pub, Jason rode the elevator to the 33rd floor. The receptionist was absent from his desk, so Jason walked freely to Grace's office.

She lifted her head when he entered, but her face remained serious.

"You must have had quite a night with Brooklyn because you made quite an impression on Aaron," she said.

"What are you talking about?" Jason said quickly.

"I saw him this morning," Grace said. "He thinks you're my boyfriend and wants us to go out together."

"What?" Jason stopped. "I don't understand."

"You don't understand?" Grace elevated her voice. "You went on a date with a girl who has been with the same guy for six years and is about to be engaged. She couldn't exactly tell him she had a great time with you."

"Brooklyn said she had a great time?" Jason said with a smile.

"Be serious, we're in trouble," Grace said plainly.

"We'll be fine," Jason said. "We will play our parts accordingly and he won't know anything different."

"It doesn't bother you that you might be sitting across the table from Aaron?" Grace said.

"We'll live in the lie," Jason said. "I'll be next to Brooklyn and we'll both be fine."

"No, I'm not a part of this," Grace said. "I won't let you destroy what she has with Aaron."

"If you don't go along with it, it'll make everything in my life worse," Jason said.

After he left Grace's office with the two in agreement, Jason was excited about another night with Brooklyn. He wanted to have Aaron alongside of him so Brooklyn could compare the two. He believed he possessed superior qualities.

Before leaving Great American Insurance's office, Jason stopped at the unattended receptionist's desk. He placed scotch tape under the sensor of his mouse and colored it with a black marker.

It'll take a man his age a few hours to figure out what's wrong with his mouse.

Just as the receptionist appeared, Jason walked out of the office as he waved to him. He returned to his desk on the 27th floor and slowly waited for the end of the day.

As he walked to his car, he was tempted to call Brooklyn about their second scheduled date with Grace and Aaron, but he didn't want to be too eager. Instead, he walked to a Walgreens several blocks away to purchase a prepaid cell phone. He paid with cash to reduce any trail of his purchase.

It was less than a week away from the shortest day of the year, so Jason walked back toward his car with the late winter sun setting on him.

27

Since Jason lived alone in his apartment, it was easy for Brooklyn to come by without any intrusions or interruptions. She'd arrive unnoticed and make her way in before any of Jason's other neighbors had an idea that a visitor had entered his apartment.

After their first date, Jason and Brooklyn didn't communicate for two weeks because of the bustle of the holiday season. They both veered in separate ways with responsibilities to family and friends.

Jason would sit in his apartment during his time off hoping that Brooklyn would text him. Day after day, he was disappointed she didn't, and he ended up chatting with Megan out of boredom. He kept up with Megan during the holidays but avoided meeting her family or creating an opportunity for her to meet him. Jason spent two weeks waiting for Brooklyn to call or text him, but she never did.

Once the New Year had passed, Jason couldn't wait any longer. After a dentist appointment on a cold January morning with flurries falling from the grey sky, Jason sped with eagerness to Brooklyn's office parking lot, waiting for her to arrive.

When she pulled in, Jason walked to her car and met her as she got out of it.

"What are you doing here?" Brooklyn said without a hint of friendliness.

"I have a belated Christmas present for you," Jason said, revealing a prepaid cell phone. "It has one phone number in it. We don't have to worry about anyone seeing us texting on our regular phones."

"You're right," Brooklyn said. "We don't have to worry about it because we aren't going to be communicating on any phone."

A week went by after Jason gave her the phone, but a text message finally did come. Brooklyn kept the phone hidden in her glove compartment and was cautious when she did use it. Jason and Brooklyn would both delete their messages and call history as soon as a conversation ended. Any calls Brooklyn made to Jason were done in the secrecy of her car.

Following a week of texting and several phone calls, Brooklyn arrived at Jason's apartment on a Tuesday night. Aaron was held late at work and Brooklyn left early, so she had several hours to spend with Jason without raising suspicion.

Finding a mutual time to meet was difficult, but after a few encounters, they were able to consistently see each other a few times a week. Brooklyn was careful to keep her interactions with Jason sporadic enough so Aaron wouldn't notice her disappearances. Megan rarely questioned anything Jason did, so concealing the meeting with Brooklyn wasn't any trouble.

The first few times Brooklyn and Jason met alone in

his apartment were uncomfortable. They hadn't spent time together in a secluded apartment without any stimulation or distraction from the outside world. But at their third meeting, the two finally became physically intimate. It was sensual and in unison, it was a slow and a hesitant harmony that was seemingly poetic, further igniting their attraction to each other.

Afterwards, the two would often lay naked in bed discussing their ambitions, worldly observations and broad theories for life. It was more than a physical attraction - Brooklyn and Jason were also intellectually connected.

Throughout the work week, Brooklyn found excuses to walk to her car during work to check her phone for messages from Jason. Their secret interactions continued for over a month as February nearly reached its halfway point.

One weekend, Jason found himself invited to a party at Julie's house, and having spent most of his free time with Brooklyn, he hadn't seen his friends in a while. He decided to go so they wouldn't start prying even more into his private life. By 10 p.m., everyone from the usual group had arrived. The party started slow, but more than 20 people filled the house around midnight.

Megan wouldn't leave Jason's side as he walked around the crowd socializing with friends.

"What are you two planning for your first Valentine's Day as a couple?" one of Julie's friends asked.

The question made Jason cringe, but Julie's friend wasn't

the only one asking that question to the seemingly happy couple.

Jason made his way to Naomi and Brandon who were cornered in the living room.

"Did you invite anyone here?" Brandon asked.

"Yeah, they're on their way," Jason said.

Several more people walked in as the crowd stretched to take in more guests.

Julie had been given her parents' old house years ago. She lived just far enough away from her neighbors that the sounds coming from inside the home weren't a disturbance. People began to sprawl into the basement and back porch. But the crowd's noise and craziness seemed to be growing.

"Don't you think this is getting a little out of hand, maybe we should slow down," Jason said when he saw Julie in the basement.

"Let them have fun for a little longer," Julie said. "We'll get them out eventually."

Jason returned upstairs as he heard Julie scream, "You broke the fan!"

He found Megan talking with a circle of people. She complimented him, which started playful banter back and forth. Jason and Megan continued to hold the attention of the small circle as smiles and laughs were shared because of the couple's apparent chemistry.

Jason and Megan moved to the picture window in the kitchen that looked over at the crowd on the back porch. The couple talked for a few minutes while observing the crowd outside, but eventually turned their attention back inside.

New faces filled the living room as the house was overrun with people. Distracted by the crowd, Jason and Megan were being approached by Ashley and Brad.

"Jason!" Ashley said as he and Megan turned.

"It's Brooklyn, right?" Brad extended his hand to Megan. "We met that night a while ago."

Megan returned his question with a confused look before staring at Jason, who was trying to recover from the mistake.

"Megan, this is Brad and Ashley," Jason said. "We work together at the Business Weekly."

The two couples spoke for a few minutes, but Megan pulled Jason away from the conversation.

Her eyes are searing into me.

"Why did they call me Brooklyn?" Megan demanded.

"It's just a mistake," Jason said. "They haven't met you before."

"But they've met Brooklyn with you before," Megan said. "They've seen you together."

"I think they were just confused," Jason said.

"Confused!" Megan emphasized. "What I'm not confused about is that I had a roommate named Brooklyn who you couldn't look away from whenever she was around."

"What are you talking about?" Jason said frustratedly. "I met her once at a party. Do you really think I went out of my way to find her?"

Jason didn't allow Megan to answer.

"You're being ridiculous. He made a random mistake."

"If I went to ask Brad why he called me Brooklyn, what reason would he give me?" Megan said as tears began to well in her eyes.

If you lie, you must be willing to live in that lie for the rest of your life. You have to be willing to see it through until the end to live in a lie.

"Okay, go ask, he'll say it was a mistake," Jason said.

It's a 50-50 shot that Ashley and Brad will go along with my story. It just depends on how Megan phrases it; they know me well enough to cover for me.

Jason couldn't control the outcome of what would happen once Megan went up to Brad, so he did what he did best. He stepped out of the front door and ran.

The frigid night air ripped through his button-down shirt, but he ran further and further. He could feel the winter wind overwhelm his chilled body. He listened to his breath and footsteps while he looked up at the night stars. Houses passed by and Jason was out of sight from Julie's house. He'd been running for several minutes when he stopped to catch his breath in a sparse subdivision.

He thought of turning around, but he couldn't. He didn't want to face what would happen if he turned around. Once one person knew about his relationship with Brooklyn, everyone would know. Their secrecy would be destroyed and their relationships ruined.

He stood under the night sky thinking of what to do next.

After a few minutes, the winter air had chilled Jason enough. A figure in the distance walked toward him.

Julie waited until they were several feet away before speaking.

"What did you do Jason?" she said.

"What do you mean?" Jason said.

"I have a girl in my bedroom crying because of you and I want to know why," Julie said.

Jason shook his head, "You know who I am."

Julie caught herself before saying anything else to scold Jason, thinking for a moment.

"I'm sad for you, Jason," she said. "You're too restless, your life is going to be spent running if you don't slow down."

"I don't know how," Jason said apologetically.

"Stop all your searching and wanting more of everything," she said. "Nothing is ever enough for you. You are never content with where you are."

"I know," Jason said.

"Why can't you be happy?" Julie said. "Why can't you allow yourself to be happy?"

"If I could answer that question, I don't think I would be who I am," he said.

Julie grabbed Jason's arm and told him he needed to return to the party. As the two made the slow walk back to Julie's house, Jason prepared for an impending argument.

Once inside, the crowd remained heavy throughout the house, but Heather and Naomi pointed him toward Julie's bedroom. Megan sat hunched over on the bed in tears. Jason watched her cry with no sympathy, and then walked into the room.

"How could you do this to me?" Megan said. "What was so wrong with me, what didn't I do?"

No words could come to Jason's mind, so he sat quietly and shook his head. With tears running down her face, Megan looked up at Jason, who stared blankly at the carpet.

"I don't know what to do," Megan said.

"Megan, this isn't what you think it is," Jason said.

"Stop," Megan said. "I just need time to think. I'm so mad at you, and I'm disappointed in her. We lived together."

"If you give me a chance to explain, it will make sense to you," Jason said.

"Then I want you to explain all of it right now," Megan tensely said.

Live in the lie.

"Her company was a client of mine, Stanberry and I took her boss and her out to dinner to go over some ideas," Jason continued. "After we finished, we had both parked close to each other; we stopped for coffee on the way back. That was it. Nothing else happened."

"And if I asked Brooklyn about it, she would tell me the exact same thing?" Megan said.

Live in the lie.

"Yes," Jason firmly said. "It was strictly for business."

"Why didn't you tell me about it then?" she said.

"Because I didn't think it would matter, I was just doing my job," Jason said.

"You just don't tell me anything, I never know what you're doing," she said.

"I know, and I'm sorry," Jason said. "I'm going to start being more open with you."

Megan believed his lies enough to stop asking questions.

The two walked out of the bedroom and returned to the party, all detriment to their relationship washed away by Jason's straight-faced falsehoods. Jason was relieved to avoid the crisis. He went into the kitchen to make another drink.

From across the room, Naomi shook her head at Jason. He shrugged back indifferently.

The crowd eventually subsided and Jason went back to his apartment with Megan. The couple's relationship was no different than what it was when the night started.

Before falling asleep next to Megan, Jason checked his prepaid phone one final time to see if Brooklyn had sent him anything that night. With an empty message inbox and zero missed calls, Jason turned off the phone and fell asleep.

28

egan had completely forgotten the Friday night argument by Valentine's Day. Jason reaffirmed her faith by giving his best effort for the romantic holiday. He didn't intend to glorify Valentine's Day, but he had always understood the romantic opportunities it presented.

In one night, I can return to Megan's good graces by playing along with the social expectations of Valentine's Day: an Instagram post, a few flowers, anything that can be spread on social media. It's a holiday drummed up by Hallmark to boost first-quarter sales.

Jason and Brooklyn didn't text or call each other until a week after Valentine's Day. Brooklyn's message was urgent when they reconnected. Aaron had made dinner reservations for Brooklyn, Grace, Jason and himself. When Brooklyn met at Jason's apartment in a panic, he rehearsed with her how the evening would unfold.

"It's a balancing act," Jason said to her. "Both of us need to be comfortable together in front of Aaron."

Grace didn't know that Jason and Brooklyn had continued their relationships beyond their first date, so they agreed to withhold the truth from her to avoid adding more pressure to the night.

On the afternoon of the date, Jason visited Grace's office to reassure her of the plan.

"For one night, I get to be wrapped around the arms of Jason Vaughn," Grace smiled. "Isn't that every girl's dream?"

Jason didn't stop to smile at her comment and continued to instruct Grace on the expectations for the night. Jason wanted her to be as equally scripted and poised as him, their lies creating a bond together.

Before he left, Grace asked, "Why are you doing all this?"

"We need to be safe tonight," Jason said. "Everything has to go according to plan."

"Look, I made the mistake of setting you guys up," Grace said. "But that was just one night, let it go."

"Please play your part and everything will be all right for us," Jason ordered.

He left her office and returned to the 27th floor. He remained quiet at his cubicle as he anxiously waited for the workday to end. He drew cartoon figures and forged signatures of famous people on scrap paper. He watched the clock slowly tick into the afternoon. When the clock inched past four, Jason had enough. He packed his things and went to the elevator.

When the elevator doors opened, Grace stood in the corner. The two looked at each other for a moment, but didn't speak as the elevator traveled to the first-floor lobby. Their scripted lie that was set to start in a few hours destroyed their natural flow of elevator small talk as they went their separate ways.

Jason extended his workout routine longer than usual to prepare for the evening out. He wanted his entire mind to be consumed with making it on time rather than the actual encounter with Brooklyn and Aaron, together.

He chose his best suit jacket along with new shoes before driving to Grace's house. Grace and Jason rode together to Brooklyn and Aaron's house, where the four planned to leave in one car.

As Jason pulled into the driveway, Brooklyn and Aaron walked outside to meet the other couple.

"I'm Aaron," he said, firmly shaking Jason's hand. "Grace finally found a good match."

He doesn't remember me from the bar.

"Yeah, I guess so," Jason said nervously. "Jason Vaughn."

"Brooklyn, you've met Jason before," Grace said.

Jason and Brooklyn awkwardly stared at each other before Aaron broke the silence that seemed to last too long.

"I'll drive us," Aaron said.

"Jason, why don't you sit up front with me?" Aaron said. "I've been wanting to meet the guy that's been taking my girl from me."

How could he know?

"Grace used to always be spending time with us," Aaron continued as Jason sat stiffly in the front passenger seat. "We never see her anymore. You must be keeping her busy."

Jason softly laughed and turned back to Grace for help in starting a conversation.

The lights of downtown appeared as Aaron drove onto Main Street.

"Where are we going tonight?" Grace asked.

With a smile on his face, Aaron shared the destination with the other three riders.

"It's a special place," he said. "It took me almost a month to get a table there, Linzio's on Main. I wanted it to be a surprise for all of you."

Jason glanced at Brooklyn, who shared a worried look with him. Linzio could expose everything with one brief stop at the table. Linzio would assume Jason and Brooklyn had brought another couple along with them for a return visit.

While following Aaron into the restaurant, Jason and Brooklyn shared a final look of dismay before their scripted evening took a turn for the worse.

Though Grace already knew part of the secret Jason and Brooklyn shared, Jason realized as he walked to the table that his affair with Brooklyn was about to be exposed. Besides Megan's doubt that had been quickly shoved aside by lies, Jason's relationship with Brooklyn had been perfectly crafted in secrecy. He worried that the exposition of their affair would ruin his connection with Brooklyn. The privacy of their relationship had enthralled both of them.

After being seated, a different waiter from their first date arrived at the table. While the four shared a bottle of wine, Jason tried to casually scan the restaurant for Linzio, but couldn't find the old man hovering around tables or sitting at the bar.

The anxiety of their relationship being discovered had forced Jason and Brooklyn into unnerving silence. Aaron and Grace carried the table's conversation. With nervousness pumping into Jason's body, he noticed the waiter walk into the restroom. He excused himself and followed the man inside.

"Here, take this," Jason said as he handed the waiter $40. "You *have* to make sure Linzio doesn't come to our table tonight. I don't want him to even see us."

"Sir, he won't be at the restaurant tonight," the waiter said confusedly.

Jason exhaled deeply before returning to the table and acted a bit dejected. Then he said, "Linzio is off tonight. I thought he might be here." Brooklyn's tension eased while Aaron naively continued to enjoy the evening.

After spending a bit of time with Aaron, Jason understood why Brooklyn was attracted to him. Aaron was well-mannered and sociable, presenting himself well and was seemingly able to gain approval from anyone around him, but he was so bland.

Once the table had been cleared after dinner, Jason believed the secret could continue. But before the waiter could bring the check, Grace and Brooklyn both asked for coffee.

"I'll bring out a pot," the waiter said.

The four sat at the table for another 20 minutes as Brooklyn and Grace drank coffee. Jason impatiently watched the two women finish their cups.

Jason knew Aaron would want to pay for the entire table's

dinner, so he had alerted the waiter earlier in the evening that he would take the check. Jason didn't want Brooklyn to think he couldn't cover their dinner. Jason couldn't control when or if Aaron would find out about the affair or how long Brooklyn would be interested in continuing their secret relationship, but for one night, he wanted to be able to pay for her dinner free of consequences.

The waiter told the four that the bill had been covered when Aaron asked for the check. He happily accepted the gift, but Brooklyn drew her eyes toward Jason to show she realized what he had done.

"It must have been a rich, older person," Aaron said. "My grandfather used to buy young couple's dinners when he was out by himself."

After the four stood up from the table in the middle of the dining area, Grace paced a few steps ahead of Jason and Brooklyn while Aaron followed a few steps behind.

Ahead of the other three, Grace passed through the door into the cold night air while it was held open for her. After holding the door for Grace, an older man walked in and removed his hat.

He looked up with a bright smile on his face as Brooklyn, Jason and Aaron moved toward him several steps away.

"The night I don't come in, you two come back," Linzio excitedly said. "I'm so glad I stopped by for a moment."

Linzio had arrived at his restaurant moments before it was set to close for the night. Struck by the lie the two had lived for the past six weeks, Jason and Brooklyn struggled to say anything with half-smiles on their faces as Aaron stood directly behind them.

"Jason, how are you?" Linzio asked sincerely. "Brooklyn, I couldn't have asked for a prettier face to come in tonight."

Jason smiled and spoke with Linzio for a few moments as Brooklyn and Aaron walked past the two. Linzio noticed several other patrons and excused himself as Brooklyn, Aaron and Grace stood outside.

Jason didn't want to think about what would come next. He looked around the restaurant knowing he could always remember the night before and after it was ruined. The evening would be devoured by infamy when he walked outside, but he had to move forward.

"Why the hell did that man say you both were together here before?" Aaron asked at Brooklyn with growing anger as Jason stepped outside.

Live in the lie.

Before Brooklyn could say anything, Jason returned to his rehearsed line he had used with Megan several weeks ago.

"It was for business," Jason said. "We went to dinner here, my agency paid for it. My boss came with us."

Aaron turned to Brooklyn.

"So, when I asked a few weeks ago if you had ever been here before, did it slip your mind?"

"No," Brooklyn pleaded. "I wanted to go here with you. I didn't want a business dinner to count for me coming to this place."

Jason was impressed with Brooklyn's ability to extend his initial lie.

Aaron didn't accept what either of the two said, pressing further.

"So, if call your boss and will all this check out," Aaron said.

"Aaron, stop, that's unnecessary," Brooklyn said.

"What is his name?" Aaron demanded of Brooklyn. "The man you met here."

Jason didn't give Brooklyn time to respond.

"Charles Stanberry. He's my boss."

Aaron turned to Grace, "Did you know anything about this?"

Grace shook her head to deny any knowledge of it.

The 15-minute car ride was silent. Jason stared at the night sky as Grace sat next to him in the back seat.

When the car arrived back at Aaron and Brooklyn's house, Jason and Grace returned to his car. He watched as Aaron and Brooklyn walked into the house. He was unsure of what would happen in the house that night, but looked inside before he drove Grace back to her house.

They sat in silence until the end of the ride.

"I told you all of this would blow up on you," Grace said.

"Nothing has blown up," Jason answered. "I'm going to get to Stanberry tomorrow before Aaron calls and everything'll be fine."

"You're going to have your boss lie for you?" Grace asked.

"Yes," Jason said firmly.

"So how deep does this go?" Grace said. "How many more people are you going to encircle with your lies? It's more than just me now."

"I'll go as far with it as possible," Jason said. "These lies have me with Brooklyn, so I like where I am."

"Jason, you can't do this anymore," Grace said. "It's always going to end the same way, whether it's today, tomorrow or next week. This whole thing ends badly for Brooklyn and you."

When they reached Grace's house, she tapped him on the back on the shoulder and left him alone in the car. Instead of driving back to his apartment, Jason returned to Brooklyn's house to look through the windows one more time.

The lights were out and both cars were parked in the driveway. Jason couldn't see any signs of distress or destruction, so he drove away.

He wanted to go back to his apartment, but he realized the lifeline of his relationship with Brooklyn Turner rested in the hands of Charles Stanberry. Jason drove downtown and parked a few blocks away from his office building.

He checked in with the security guard in the first-floor lobby, who granted him access to the elevators. Jason rode up the elevator to an empty and dark 27th floor past midnight. He followed his usual footsteps to his cubicle before going into Stanberry's unlocked office. After looking around the office of the man he despised more than anyone, Jason took off his suit jacket and lay down on Stanberry's couch.

The quiet office hummed over the sporadic noises on the street below. Jason closed his eyes for a few moments, but eventually checked both of his phones to see if Brooklyn had sent anything to him. Both phones were blank, leaving the relationship in question until tomorrow morning.

Jason drifted off to sleep knowing the peril he would face at sunrise, but for the night, he could still win Brooklyn Turner.

29

As the morning sun began to rise over the horizon, Jason rose up from his incoherent state with a sore back and ungroomed hair. Lights around the office flicked on as people shuffled in for the final day of the work week. Jason could hear people talking, so he went to close Stanberry's partially opened door.

Lights continued to turn on around the office. Stanberry would arrive at his usual time, so Jason took a few moments to fix his appearance. He took a bottle of water to freshen his hair and face. He moved around the room, tightening up his clothes and attempting to thrust some semblance of life into his body.

Even his eyes felt tired, but Jason noticed a blue note on the edge of Stanberry's desk that read "MRI 9:30."

X-rays and MRIs aren't how I want to spend my mornings.

It had little meaning to Jason other than Stanberry's arrival would be delayed. Instead of being able to debrief Stanberry on the previous night's events by nine, Jason would have to wait in an empty office for hours. The workspace was filled enough that Jason couldn't leave Stanberry's empty office without some suspicion from coworkers.

Suddenly a knock tapped on Stanberry's door, but went away a few moments later. The office patterns of the 27th floor rarely changed, so Jason worried about the absence of himself and Stanberry at the same time.

When Stanberry opened his door a few minutes after 11 a.m., he was startled to see Jason sitting across from his desk.

"You're the last person I expected to see here," Stanberry said.

"Where have you been?" Jason asked.

"Doctor's appointment," Stanberry paused.

"Your note said you had to get an MRI," Jason pointed to the desk.

"Yeah," Stanberry said raising his eyebrow. "They think I have a malignant tumor in my head."

I can't deal with a full breakdown of his health problems right now. There's a reason I've been here so long.

"You'll be all right, doctors know what they're doing," Jason said. "Did you receive any calls today?"

"No," Stanberry said.

"Well, I need your help. There might be one today," Jason said. "I need to make sure we're on the same page."

"What're you talking about?"

"This guy is going to call and ask if you went to dinner with a woman and me," Jason said. "I told him it was a business dinner, that she was a client of ours."

"So, you want me to lie for you?" Stanberry asked.

"It isn't like that," Jason explained. "All you have to say is that you were at a dinner with us and it was strictly business. Everything else will take care of itself."

"If it was strictly for business, you wouldn't be coming to me for help," Stanberry said. "I realize what's going on."

"I came to you because I knew you could help me, I need this one thing more than anything else," Jason said. "I'm calling in everything I've ever done for you to help with this one favor."

Stanberry calmly looked at Jason.

"Jason, I'm not as talented as you and I never will be, but when I go back to my family every night, I know they're seeing an honorable man," Stanberry said. "And since they believe that, I'm okay with not having all the talent or money that other people have, but what you're doing isn't honorable and I don't think you'll be able to live with it."

"This is different," Jason pleaded. "I need this."

"I won't do it," Stanberry said firmly. "If this man calls and asks questions, I'm going to answer them as honestly as I can because I try to be an honest man."

"You want to stick it to me that badly," Jason said.

"I'm not sticking it to you," Stanberry said. "I've watched you grow up these last few years like you're my own son, but what you're doing now, it's wrong."

Jason shook his head and left Stanberry's office with frustration as his face grew red with anger. He knew Aaron would be able to break through the light seal of lies that had protected Brooklyn and him.

Waiting helplessly at his desk for a phone call he had no

control over, Jason devoted his entire attention to listening for the phone to ring in Stanberry's office. He tried closing his eyes to rest from the uncomfortable night.

Jason met Keshawn for lunch to avoid any unnecessary torment. He passed Stanberry's office around noon, the aging superior shaking his head in disapproval. During lunch, Jason decided against sharing any of the recent drama with Keshawn simply to get a short reprieve. The two young men took their time eating lunch, but Jason couldn't stop time and eventually had to head back to work.

He arrived back at his office building and rode the elevator to the 33rd floor. He walked by the receptionist's desk to Grace's office. For the first time, she was callous with him.

"I haven't heard anything, and I won't be asking for you either," Grace said. "You want somebody to tell you you're doing the right thing, and I won't be the one to give you that reassurance."

Jason couldn't disagree with her, so he left her office with no information or encouragement. He sulked at his cubicle for the remainder of the afternoon. He returned to Stanberry's office around five as the man that held control of his relationship with Brooklyn prepared to leave.

"I never got a phone call today," Stanberry said. "So whatever mess you got yourself into, the storm never came."

Jason nodded his head, pleased that he could leave the office with his tightly manicured life intact.

"But Jason, before you go," Stanberry paused. "I want you to know there will come a time when you have to atone for your mistakes. Take it from me, it is better to be truthful and do the right thing than fall down the wrong path."

If only Stanberry could realize that the right path is Brooklyn Turner. If only everyone could see that none of this is a mistake, then they'd support me, support us.

Though no one had reassured him about his relationship with Brooklyn, Jason needed to reassure himself.

"One day, everything will make sense and you'll know I did what I was supposed to do," Jason said.

With a touch of spring in the late February air, Jason walked to his car parked a few blocks away assured that everything was fine between Brooklyn and Aaron, which meant everything was fine between him and Brooklyn. Their secret could live on.

When he returned to his apartment, Jason collapsed on his bed. He slept for a few hours until his phone rang.

"Hello?"

"Jason, where were you last night?"

Jason listened to Ashley expunge her disapproval of his absence at Business Weekly the night before, when he was supposed to be wrapping up his final corrections.

"I waited for you to come do your edits, but you never did," Ashley said. "What was going on last night? You're the one person we can always count on."

"I'm so sorry," Jason apologized. "It just slipped my mind."

"What's going on...nothing ever just slips your mind," Ashley said.

"Nothing's, I just got busy and forgot. I'm sorry," Jason said.

"Well you're too consistent and reliable for that to happen again, so I assume I'll be seeing you next week," Ashley said.

Jason hung up the phone in disappointment. Though seemingly everyone around him had disapproved of his actions the past several weeks, the Business Weekly staff's image of him had remained untarnished. This mishap would bring doubt into those coworkers' minds.

Frustration was building inside of him, but before he had time to calm himself down, he received another phone call moments after placing his phone on the countertop.

"Yes?"

"Jason?"

He didn't recognize the phone number when he answered, but he knew it was Brooklyn's voice.

"I told him everything," she said.

"What do you mean?" Jason said.

"Everything," Brooklyn paused. "I told Aaron everything. I couldn't live with this anymore. I couldn't keep it from him any longer."

Jason could feel his body plummet internally.

"Why...why'd you do that?" he asked.

"After last night, I had to," Brooklyn said.

After believing the crisis had been avoided just hours before, Jason knew then that his time with Brooklyn Turner was officially ending.

"Jason, I don't know what we were doing," Brooklyn said.

"You were the only person that could ever distract me from Aaron, but my life is with him and I'm going to work through all this with him."

"Why did you call to tell me this?" Jason said. "I'd rather you just dropped me."

As Brooklyn sighed and collected her thoughts, Jason walked into his bedroom and grabbed a small bag from his closet. He carried it out to his car while still on the phone.

"I wanted you to know, I didn't want you to think anything besides the truth," Brooklyn said. "This had to stop."

The moment a man can feel everything slipping away is when he fights the hardest.

Jason had never fought through any of his problems, he had run from them. He listened to Brooklyn talk as he weaved his car through the road. He asked Brooklyn about what Aaron said when he found out the truth and how she planned to mend her relationship with him.

He continued to ask questions to keep her on the phone. He could sense the conversation was ending when she asked, "What were you expecting from all this?"

Holding the phone in his hand, Jason skid his car to a stop and jumped out. In the darkness of night, he ran through suburban front yards and rushed into a backyard. He hopped over a small chain linked fence into another backyard.

"I was expecting you," Jason said with shortness of breath.

He looked up at Brooklyn on her back patio as she dropped her phone to her side, gazing at him. With a smile on her face, she shook her head as Jason panted.

She stepped closer to him and whispered, "You can't be here. Aaron's inside."

Jason glanced inside the house, but didn't see a silhouette or any sign of another person.

"If you didn't want me to be here right now, you wouldn't have called me," Jason answered.

"You have to go," she demanded.

"You're right," he said. "But you need to come with me."

"Jason, you know I can't," Brooklyn said.

"You're willing to live the rest of your life with this thought that you passed on someone who you were fascinated by," Jason said. "And that might not seem like an issue, but what happens when you're 35, living a content life, with the thought resting in the back of your mind that you could have had something better. You'll love your children and Aaron, but you'll always wonder what your other life could have been like. If you come with me, you won't ever have to wonder."

Brooklyn softly smiled, but shook her head.

"How does it make me look?" she said. "With everyone knowing I just tossed aside my boyfriend of six years for a guy I just met. How am I going to handle it?"

"You won't have to; there is nothing here for us," Jason said. "We will start fresh."

"Everything I have is here," Brooklyn said firmly.

"You'd be shocked how easy it is to drop everything and run," Jason answered.

"Where would we go?"

"I know exactly where we could start," he said.

Jason stared at Brooklyn. They held their eyes together until Brooklyn looked down.

"When would we leave?" she said.

"Right now," Jason said. "Get what you need. I'm parked on the road behind here. I'll meet you out there in a few minutes."

Brooklyn nodded her head and Jason vanished into the darkness of the backyard. When Jason returned to his car, he checked the clock. The next 10 minutes felt like the longest of his life. With every second that Brooklyn didn't appear, he felt himself sink lower and lower.

The tension of time ballooned to illicit proportions with each second slamming down like a hammer. Desperation had reached him.

Where is Brooklyn Turner?

He thought of returning to her backyard, but worried she would arrive at the car when he was gone. He sat in his car and waited. The minutes turned to hours and Jason's pursuit of Brooklyn had become darker than the night sky.

He started to drift to sleep around two. He had no intention of giving up, so he fell asleep in his car.

The early morning sun peaked through the clouds near the horizon as Jason started to awake. He was jolted by a sharp banging on his windshield.

An elderly man with a broom stick peered inside the car.

"Hey buddy, you can't stay here, you got to get moving," the elderly man yelled.

Jason waved his hand and slowly nodded his head, realizing

that the collapse of Jason Vaughn and Brooklyn Turner was nearly complete.

The man looked off into the distance, nodded his head and looked back at Jason.

"Sorry, I didn't know you were waiting for someone," the elderly man said before walking away.

There was a tap on the passenger side window. Jason looked over to see Brooklyn standing outside of his car. She opened the door and sat down.

"I knew if you stayed until morning, you were serious," she said.

Jason had an exasperated smile, "I didn't think you were coming."

Brooklyn smiled and asked, "Where are we going?"

Jason grinned and took a deep breath before starting the engine.

With the sun slowly rising and Brooklyn Turner beside him, Jason drove to the one place on his mind.

30

The afternoon sun stretched further to their right as Jason and Brooklyn swiftly passed barren fields still yet to sprout any growth with spring still weeks away. Jason had traveled this route so many times before he remembered every oncoming slight in the road and the nearby farm that looked over the interstate. He knew the smallest details of the drive.

It had been more than seven hours when the car stopped at a gas station in Andalusia, Alabama. The small southern town hadn't changed since Jason had driven through it as a teenager with his friend's family. He had a fascination with the small town and its people who were dedicated to a habitual routine.

He would notice a group of older men eating together in the front corner of the McDonald's every time he stopped there as a child. He had wondered about the paths the men had taken to lead them to that morning ritual in such a small town.

With the journey paused as Jason filled the tank, Brooklyn asked the question that he had been waiting for as soon as he started the trip.

"So where are we really going?"

"We went through an entire tank of gas and three states and just now you're asking me where we are going?" Jason said.

"I can wait a little longer," Brooklyn laughed. "You're eventually going to drive into a body of water."

The one thing that separated Brooklyn from any other girl Jason had known was her contentment with what she already knew. She never asked Jason about his past or his regrets because she focused her attention on what he was in the present and what could be in the future.

The sun was merely a glimmer in the westward sky by the time the two had reached the Florida Mid-Bay Bridge toll booth. After handing over some spare change, Jason and Brooklyn moved beyond the high gray concrete walls to expose a view of the Choctawhatchee Bay.

"See those two high rises just before the big cluster of buildings?" Jason pointed further east. "That's where we're going."

"You have a place there?" Brooklyn doubted.

"No, but I have a key."

Jason had driven to the condo's security gate hundreds of times before, but it was the first time he posed as an imposter. He pictured this moment ever since he snatched the condo key as a teenager.

With twilight masking their identities, Jason and Brooklyn slowly pulled up to the gate.

"We're here to see Mary Paulus, condo 705 on the gulf-side building," Jason said.

"All right, go straight back and you'll see it," the security guard said before opening the gate.

The car continued driving through the complex.

"How do you know no one will be here?" Brooklyn asked.

"I don't."

The parking garage was in the basement of the 20-floor high rise. Jason was accustomed to the bustling summer crowds, but the building was relatively empty as they rode the elevator to the seventh floor.

He exited the elevator to the white hallways on the seventh floor as Brooklyn followed. Jason looked into the windows of 705's unit. The rooms were dark, so he inserted the key and wiggled the handle to open the door.

The condo was filled with darkness, but Jason knew where every light switch was placed. He walked to the balcony that rose above the beach and opened the sliding doors to smell the salt air.

After hesitantly following a few steps behind, Brooklyn joined Jason on the balcony.

"What now?" Brooklyn asked.

Jason ignored the question and kissed her before walking inside. He went into the master bedroom, a place he had only been in several times because it was always occupied by his friend's parents. He moved to the other bedroom, which he'd shared with his friend.

He laid on one of the small beds and pictured his adolescent-self wondering if he would ever share this experience with someone else. He thought of his past experiences in Destin and his attempts to share this sacred place with other people. He returned to the master bedroom, where Brooklyn was sprawled out on the bed.

Jason laid down beside her and stroked her soft hair.

"Do you want to watch the sunrise with me tomorrow?" Jason said.

"I'd like that very much," Brooklyn answered.

Brooklyn fell asleep, so Jason went to a convenience store to get food. By the time he returned, Brooklyn was asleep, so Jason didn't disturb her.

I think better when it's late at night. I don't know why. Maybe because when I was a kid, my parents were always asleep late at night. It's not like I was afraid to think when I was around them, but there was something freeing about having my mind to myself. I think best when I'm by myself. My mind isn't busy pretending to be someone when no one else is around. Just think of it, when I'm around people, part of my mind, whether it be a large or small percentage, is dedicated to remaining in a carefully crafted character.

He found a legal pad of paper in the kitchen and began to write. In the dimly lit condo with the echoing waves crashing beneath him, Jason wrote. It had been months since he last had time to open his thoughts and get them on the page, but he finally wrote again. The ocean air helped him get ideas onto the page.

He'd been writing for a few hours when Brooklyn walked out of the bedroom and waved him to come to bed. Before falling asleep, Jason set an alarm so the two could be up before the sunrise.

The night passed quickly, but the shrill alarm wasn't necessary for the two to be ready before the sunrise. With darkness still showering over the horizon and ocean, Jason and Brooklyn made their way down to the beach.

As the two sat in the cold sand facing eastward, the cool ocean wind cut through their bodies. Jason felt alive sitting next to Brooklyn in the darkness. The sun slowly crept over the horizon. High rises and sand dunes blocked its connection with the lone two observers on the beach, but only for a few brief moments. The pinkish clouds blended with the sun as it rose over the beach to signify the beginning of the day.

"I always imagined watching this sunrise with you, ever since I was a child," Jason said.

"You didn't even know who I was eight months ago," Brooklyn said.

"But I had a vision of who you'd be, and I knew when I saw you first that's who you were," he said.

"What are we doing here, Jason?" Brooklyn said.

"The ocean," Jason paused. "It washes away everything. It is the one constant I've always had. I wanted to come here first so we could wash everything off."

"We both have to work on Monday," Brooklyn said. "We can't just disappear and drop everything."

"Yes, we can," Jason pleaded. "There isn't anything we need there. I brought plenty of money and we can build a new life here."

Brooklyn shook her head.

"I came with you because I wanted to know more about you. I wanted to know if you were running from something or searching for something. I think you're running from yourself. I don't think you want to be Jason Vaughn anymore."

"I don't," Jason said plainly.

Jason leaned back into the sand.

"My whole life I've watched people happily enjoying life and I always wondered when a moment of contentment would come for me. But no matter how hard I tried, I could never feel the way other people did about life," Jason said. "I learned to put on a fake smile and drift through supposedly big moments in my life, but I felt nothing. And then you came along and I felt that feeling that everyone else said they had and I didn't have to pretend anymore."

Brooklyn softly stretched her arm around Jason and smiled.

"It's your irrational pursuit of uninhibited happiness," Brooklyn said. "I can't be solely responsible for your self-acceptance."

The two fell back on the sand and tilted their heads to watch the sunrise. Jason couldn't think of a better moment in his life.

After the sun had moved high enough for other beach goers to start heading closer to the water, Jason and Brooklyn returned to the condo.

Without asking Jason, Brooklyn emailed her boss to tell

him she would be out of the office for a few days. Then she told Jason she needed to be back by Wednesday.

Jason agreed. He wanted to contest her decision, but realized the only way of holding onto Brooklyn for longer than their spontaneous trip was to return to Louisville. He worried about what would happen when they returned. He had expended all his energy on his pursuit of Brooklyn, but now, his relationship with her was more than a casual secret.

Though the ocean was too cold and the weather too moderate, Jason and Brooklyn made their way to the sparsely populated beach each morning to watch the sunrise.

When they were in the condo, he lived in constant fear. The thought that at any moment the owner or renters could open the door enlivened the trip. They kept their belongings near the door in case they were forced to rush out if an unannounced guest arrived.

Jason showed Brooklyn everywhere he had grown fond of during his childhood while with his friend on family vacations.

On the last night, Jason returned to his note pad again. He looked out from the balcony and saw the moon reflecting over the dark waves. He could feel himself give into the flow of his own writing, his pen and mind moving simultaneously to the rhythm of his thoughts.

After leaving under the shadow of the corporate ladder, Jason found time to write. The monotonous corporate lifestyle had disrupted his ability to craft and cultivate words. He had found a place where he could write undisturbed. After reaching a stopping point, Jason walked into the bedroom, where Brooklyn lay back reading a book.

Jason marveled at her beauty as she intently read.

"One day, you'll read one of my books," Jason said.

She looked up.

"What will it be about?" she asked.

"You," he said.

To keep their inevitable tension at bay, the two joined together as the waves crashed upon the sand in the distance.

31

She awoke to the sun squinting through the white curtains with Jason beside her.

A text message from Aaron asking where she was waited for her response as she gently pulled off the white sheets. She looked over at Jason, wondering what was going through his mind as they prepared to return to Louisville.

After packing her small bag, she checked to see if Jason was ready to leave. He nodded and they unceremoniously left the condo for the final time.

While Jason went to the parking garage to get the car, Brooklyn walked to the beach to see the sand and ocean one final time. She could feel the cold sand in between her feet send shivers up her body while the morning breeze lightly moved across her face. The morning sun glistened beautifully on the blue green water while Brooklyn scanned the beach for any other observers.

In the last week, Brooklyn's entire life had changed, and she had no idea what she'd be returning home to this evening.

She didn't even know what home *was* anymore. She hadn't spoken to Aaron since the night before she left with Jason, but she assumed he'd still be living at their house. All her things were there, so she had no place to go to get space from him.

She began thinking that starting a new life was the truly the best choice as Jason said before, but she couldn't imagine disappearing indefinitely from her family and job. She'd been so close to Aaron for the past six years, she wanted him to know why she'd suddenly called things off.

Though Brooklyn was intrigued by Jason's undefined future, she wasn't sure what would happen next and that bothered her. Jason had lived with frustrating and inconclusive endings his entire life, but Brooklyn wanted closure on everything before she moved forward.

The trip to Destin was good, but the thought of her future loomed as well. Jason could push away Megan with disregard, yet Brooklyn was amid a six-year relationship, during which her family and friends had become so interconnected with Aaron that he became a part of them, too.

She didn't know what they'd think of her after she escaped with Jason. She couldn't say she'd fallen in love with him, because she hadn't, but she was morbidly captivated by who he was and she didn't know why.

As the car pulled out of the complex, the Brooklyn's responsibility came closer and closer, mile by mile. She had only glanced at her phone a few times during her stay in the condo, so the drive back was the first time she scrolled through everything she had missed.

Text messages, emails, phone calls and voicemails filled her phone. One at a time, she responded to each of them. After diverting her attention from Jason, she turned to him in search of a greater understanding.

"When you were younger, what did you want to be?"

It was the first time Brooklyn ever asked Jason about his past.

"I wanted to be remembered," Jason said.

He continued.

"I wasn't fixated on an illusion of love or greed, I wanted immortality. I knew I was going to die, but I wanted my life to be passed down, for people to know my name. But nothing I could do seemed significant enough for me to be remembered, so I moved on without it."

"So, you never cared about a picturesque life, the American Dream with a wife and children?" Brooklyn asked.

"No," Jason smiled. "If I'm Jay Gatsby, my green light wasn't Daisy; it was being remembered as great."

"What changed?" she asked.

"I think I realized how meaningless everything seemed," Jason said.

"I'd disagree with you on that," Brooklyn said. "And I think you want to disagree with yourself too, because I know you don't think that's true, whether it's subconscious or something else. There's more to you than that."

Jason raised his eyebrows and tried to manicure a response, but couldn't answer. Brooklyn looked out the window and drifted into a light sleep.

The journey's final stop for gas was just north of Nashville.

Brooklyn could feel her nervousness grow as the car passed over the Kentucky-Tennessee border.

When they reached Louisville Metro's city limits, Brooklyn's problems filled her mind once again. She'd soon be walking into a house occupied by a man that she'd abandoned. She knew she had to walk through the front door and face that uncomfortable conversation, no matter the consequences.

While Brooklyn had the most challenging conversation in her young life waiting for her, Jason could return to his apartment and the life he left behind without any repercussions. Megan would already understand his dispassion and openly give up on him.

"Do you want me to go inside with you?" Jason asked as they pulled into Brooklyn's driveway.

"No," she said. "That'd be worse."

"You don't have to go in, you can come back to my apartment and we can figure out what comes next," he said.

"Jason, I have to atone for what I have done," Brooklyn said.

"Will I see you again?" Jason asked legitimately.

"I don't know," she answered.

Brooklyn reached for her small bag and opened the passenger door. She turned to look at Jason before walking to the front door.

Before going inside, she ran her hand through her hair and watched the car slowly back out of the driveway. With her hands shaking in front of her, Brooklyn fit the key into the lock and turned the doorknob.

The dimly lit living room was empty, so Brooklyn made her way to the kitchen, where Aaron sat at the table. She could see the frustration on his face.

"Where've you been?" he demanded.

She didn't defer from questions like Jason. She answered honestly.

"I was in Florida with Jason," Brooklyn said.

"Brooklyn, why'd you do this to me?" Aaron said meekly. "Am I that horrible of a person?"

"I don't know why I went," Brooklyn cried, tears already streaming down her face. "I still love you. I just wanted to go."

"You know we can't fix this now," Aaron said. "Everything is ruined."

"I know," Brooklyn admitted.

"Pack your things," Aaron said defeatedly. "You can't stay here tonight."

With tears trickling down her face, Brooklyn nodded and went into the bedroom to get as many clothes as she could fit into her car.

After Brooklyn's second trip, Aaron started to help Brooklyn take her belongings to the car. In complete silence and amidst infidelity, Aaron was still a devoted to Brooklyn. The two filled the car until nothing else could fit.

Brooklyn slid into the driver's seat as Aaron stood next to the door.

"Is what I did wrong or what he did right?" Aaron asked with tears filling his eyes.

Brooklyn held Aaron's hand and looked up at him.

"You never did anything wrong," Brooklyn said. "I was the one who wasn't content with all of this."

Aaron rubbed her hand and let it go, then closed the car door.

Brooklyn's face was filled with tears as she drove down the driveway leaving the picturesque relationship she'd once so desperately desired in the rearview mirror. As she made her way to Jason's apartment, Brooklyn thought of how she'd envisioned her life when she was a teenager.

She remembered wanting to be married to a successful husband who was deeply in love with her. She wanted to watch their careers develop and eventually have children together. She wanted to grow old with her husband, never letting a single day go by when she didn't doubt her love for him. And yet now, she was driving away from that thought. Aaron offered all of it while Jason's undefinable, wayward life couldn't guarantee any of it.

Brooklyn couldn't understand why she had passed on everything she once wanted for someone she hardly knew. She didn't need to conceal their affair anymore. Brooklyn asked Jason if she could bring some of her clothes inside. Jason told her to sit down as he carried her things into his apartment.

Brooklyn went to the bathroom to take a shower. She was unable to tell the difference between the water and the tears that dripped from her face. Overcome with guilt and pain, Brooklyn collapsed on the shower floor and sat quietly crying as the cold water speckled her body.

After a few minutes of solemn solitude, Jason found

Brooklyn crunched up on the shower floor. He turned off the water and moved beside her, cradling her in his arms.

The cold water dampened Jason's clothes, but Brooklyn and he sat interlocked on the shower floor. They had each traveled down a different path to reach this moment, but now the two were connected by what had been done.

"What now?" Brooklyn whispered.

Jason stood up and put a towel around her. He picked her up and carried her to his bed. She lay silently in the bed with her wet hair dripping onto the sheets.

Before falling asleep, she checked her phone. She looked over at Jason and once more, wondered what exactly was going on in his mind.

A text message from Aaron asking where she was lit up her phone as Brooklyn gently pulled up the white sheets around her. She fell asleep to the moon squinting through the white curtains with Jason beside her.

32

rooklyn lived at Jason's apartment for a full week. She'd returned to her job after three days off, but Jason had no urge to resume work with Creative Productions. He hadn't called or notified anyone of his absence and felt no obligation to do so. The frequent phone calls eventually subsided as Jason hoped his coworkers assumed the worst.

He imagined Stanberry bringing the team together for a speech about the life of Jason Vaughn. He laughed thinking of Stanberry telling everyone to live out the rest of their days at Creative Productions in honor of Jason.

As Jason sat in his apartment, he wondered about how many people from work would attend his funeral. He could rely on a few of his friends to fill out a few seats in the front row, but he hadn't built enough solid relationships for masses of people to attend.

A lightly attended visitation wouldn't bother Jason. He had more respect for the people who didn't attend funerals for people they didn't truly know. He stayed away from funerals himself, so why should he expect random people to take a few hours out of their day to attend the closing ceremony of his life.

Though the vision of his funeral didn't frighten him, he wondered how he'd be remembered. He questioned if there would be any eulogies or release of emotions during the ceremony. He didn't think many people shared an emotional connection with him.

Jason could only guarantee seven people at his funeral. With the thought in his mind, Jason was tempted to go along with his hypothetical disappearance to see who would join his grieving friends after he faked his death. He would sit in the far back with an ample disguise to see who valued him enough to pay their respects to his uneventful life.

The daydream subsided, allowing Jason to return to writing. Without work at Creative Productions, he wrote much more than he ever had. He scrolled further down his word document every day, adding more and more.

The original resurgence of his passion for writing merely produced a few pages of unscripted thoughts on his and Brooklyn's beach getaway, but by the time they left Destin, a direction had taken shape in his work.

Jason had decided to write a fiction book about his own experiences. It was a fictional novel that he believed would one day be placed besides books by Ernest Hemingway, F. Scott Fitzgerald and William Faulkner. He discovered his writing was the way for his legacy to continue after his death.

While Brooklyn worked, Jason wrote.

The words came together by the thousands as he raced forward with the novel. Without any social interaction during the day, Jason's mind was clearer than ever before. He didn't have to bother with the pursuit of Brooklyn Turner during the day, so his full attention could be dedicated to writing.

When Friday evening arrived, Jason and Brooklyn agreed their relationship couldn't continue without leaving the apartment. They decided to go downtown, but neither contacted their social circles.

Jason didn't know if his inconclusive ending with Megan was sitting poorly with his friends, even though he knew they would eventually invite him to another one of their parties again. He wasn't disowned, but Julie was close enough with Megan that she'd ask everyone else to stay away from Jason for a few weeks once she found out he ghosted her.

Brooklyn had lost touch with her friends during her time at Jason's apartment. Her best friends and former roommates felt betrayed by her. Brooklyn had run off with an unknown guy, abandoned Aaron and abandoned them as well.

With few people left on their side, Jason and Brooklyn made their way downtown Friday night to make their first public appearance together. They had several brief encounters with acquaintances from high school and college. The night progressed further without conflict until Jason noticed a few friends walk into the bar.

Julie and Kyle were followed by Heather, Keshawn and Naomi.

Keshawn and Jason made eye contact first. Jason motioned to Keshawn to meet near the bar as Brooklyn was talking to other people.

As the four others drifted to another part of the bar, Jason met Keshawn.

"Where the hell have you been?" Keshawn said.

"I had to get away for a little bit," Jason said.

"So, it's true, about Brooklyn and you," Keshawn asked.

"Are people upset by it?" Jason said.

"I don't think anyone cares besides Megan, she was upset," Keshawn said. "But when she is being replaced by Brooklyn Turner, I can't be mad at you."

Loyalty means more to me than forgiveness. Keshawn's always going to be on my side.

Jason and Keshawn drank together for a few minutes until Julie stepped between them, poking Jason's back.

"I wish that'd been a knife," Julie said.

Jason turned to see Kyle and Heather following Julie, who openly showed her distaste for Jason.

"I'm surprised the two biggest villains in the city are allowed out after five," Julie said.

"She isn't as mad as she is pretending to be," Kyle said to Jason, trying to diffuse any tension.

Jason didn't want to argue or defend himself to Julie, so he scanned the bar for Brooklyn. He found her standing in a corner talking to Naomi.

"She's *trying* to tell you we're glad you're back," Heather said to reassure Jason.

Keshawn slapped Jason on the back in a brotherly fashion; Heather and Kyle winked at him. It was then Jason knew the years spent with these friends meant more than his few months with Megan. Though they hadn't fully forgiven him for how he'd distastefully treated Megan, they'd welcomed him back.

The night continued as Jason circulated the bar with his friends and Brooklyn. He watched her socialize with different people. She didn't need him present nor did she want him next to her the whole time, so Jason was able to roam freely.

He waited to find Naomi alone, so he could gauge her reaction to the scandalous exodus.

"You finally found the right girl," Naomi said.

"I didn't expect to hear you admit that," Jason responded.

"My conclusion on the perfect girl for Jason Vaughn," Naomi paused. "You want a girl who can offer you greater depth into your life, but you won't ever find that, so instead, you found a girl attractive enough to distract you from craving any intellectual stimulation."

Jason pinched his eyebrows in confusion, knowing Naomi would continue to explain.

"My only question is," Naomi said. "When does all that wear off for you? Your mind is too active to be satisfied with a pretty face forever. Besides, don't you think you'll eventually become bored with her, too?"

"You doubt me more than anyone else in the world," Jason said.

"I believe in who you truly are more than anyone else in the world," Naomi answered. "I expect more from you more than anyone."

"Fair enough," Jason said. He walked away, leaving Naomi by herself in the crowded bar.

He found Brooklyn with some of her friends and listened to them talk. He was out of place standing next to Brooklyn as she talked with her friends. Aaron had stood next to her for six years. Jason could sense everyone around him wished Aaron was standing in his place.

The people giving me these looks aren't ever going to give me a true chance with her. No amount of effort can ever change their distaste for me, so I'll stand quietly, knowing I have what they don't want me to have. They can call me a coward, a cheater and a liar, but they can't take away the fact that I'm the one standing next to Brooklyn Turner.

After the crowd thinned out at 3 a.m., Brooklyn and Jason decided to leave. They didn't have an urge to say goodbye to anyone, so they left the bar. With the car parked a few blocks down the road, they made the slow walk under city lights. A homeless man moved toward the two on the same sidewalk. Jason switched places with Brooklyn to be in between her and the vagrant.

She's the first person I've ever had a strong will to protect. I usually consider unselfishness to be weak, but I like this obligation to her.

The homeless man passed the two without saying anything.

Before riding back to the apartment, Jason drove to an empty parking garage a few blocks away near the center of downtown Louisville. The car climbed the spiral ramp to the seventh-floor rooftop that overlooked the city.

"I used to look up at the stars and wonder if you were seeing the same thing," Jason said.

"It's going to be tough living here Jason," she said.

"Then let's start fresh, like I've been saying," he said.

"I don't think you need me to start fresh, but you want someone to guide you on who you should be," Brooklyn said.

"Go ahead, pick anyone and I'll be that person for you," Jason smiled.

"I'll get to pick a new character every day?" Brooklyn laughed.

"Where should we go?" Jason asked.

"Somewhere with some more lights," Brooklyn answered.

Louisville had been their only home for their entire lives, but now Jason and Brooklyn needed to be overwhelmed by a new experience to rid them of indiscretions and search for a new beginning.

33

*A*s the CEO of Creative Productions, Paul Harbaugh left his large corner office in Chicago for a week every month to check on the three other branches of his ad agency.

He traveled from Chicago to St. Louis to Louisville to Indianapolis before returning to Chicago over a three-day span once a month. He considered it necessary to feel the pulse of the company.

Harbaugh had held the position of CEO for more than five years after working his way up the corporate ladder. He led and communicated well, so he was respected and commanded an unrivaled support amongst his employees.

He decided against staying in St. Louis on a Monday night in April, instead driving straight to Louisville to spend a full day in the branch directed by James Downing. Harbaugh was informed days earlier that Louisville's prized associate Jason Vaughn had disappeared.

Though Jason had developed the initial ad campaign that attracted Audi, Creative Productions was more than capable to move on without him. After Downing told Harbaugh the news, the two jokingly agreed that 'everyone is replaceable.'

While Harbaugh walked into the 27th floor lobby of Creative Productions a little past nine, Jason rolled off his bed to prepare for the morning ahead. Brooklyn had left for work an hour earlier, but unlike the previous days of unemployment for Jason, he wouldn't spend long hours of the day writing.

As much as Jason wanted to believe Brooklyn and he could live out the rest of their youth with him writing novels and short stories, he realized none of it would be potent enough to keep Brooklyn around for long.

The cold shower water washed away Jason's freedom and once again, he became a businessman. He could feel the corporate hierarchy surrounding him as he picked out his best navy suit and a silk red tie. The familiar drive was so imprinted in his mind after three years that he believed he could drive it blindfolded.

He found a parking spot a few blocks away and walked through the city's late morning business rush into the building that housed Creative Productions. Instead of going toward the elevators to ascend to the 27th floor, Jason found a seat in the lobby and read a newspaper.

Sitting far enough away from the elevators and usual path of any Creative Productions employees, he doubted anyone would stray away from their monotonous routine to notice him.

A few minutes before 11 a.m., Jason folded the newspaper and walked to the small food stand in the lobby.

He timed it perfectly. The elevator doors opened and Paul Harbaugh walked to the food stand. The CEO was only a few feet from the stand when he noticed Jason.

"Jason Vaughn," Harbaugh said with a smile. "Everyone told me you were dead. You should have waited a few weeks to time your resurrection with Easter."

"Not dead, actually," Jason said.

"From the company's standpoint you've been dead for three weeks," Harbaugh said. "What exactly are you doing here today? Are you going to beg Downing for your job back after you left without so much as an email?"

I've worked for Creative Productions for three years observing Harbaugh's routine. Every Tuesday of the same week every month, Harbaugh arrives at our lobby just a little past nine and goes to Downing's office. He tours about the 27th and 28th floors to watch employees at work. Every Tuesday trip he makes to Louisville, he heads to the elevators just a few minutes before 11 and returns five minutes later. In my first year, I was curious where a CEO would disappear to for five minutes in a foreign building, but by my second year, I knew to wait in the lobby before he left for five minutes. Midway through year two, I knew Harbaugh was going to the first-floor lobby food stand to buy a small coffee and plain cinnamon raisin bagel.

"No, I actually wanted to talk to you," Jason said.

Harbaugh didn't hide his surprise.

"I'm not giving you your job back," Harbaugh said. "You disappeared. You abandoned everyone. We can't bring you back after that stunt."

"Do you remember how you told me you wanted me in Chicago, working on bigger projects?" Jason said.

"I'm not giving you a job in Chicago either," Harbaugh said plainly.

"No, that isn't what I want," Jason said. "This company just signed its biggest account in its history. Creative Productions is strong, but it needs more."

"We'll keep bringing in bigger and bigger accounts," Harbaugh said.

"Creative Productions needs to be in the Mecca of advertising," Jason said. "New York City. Send me up there with a skeleton staff and let's start carving out some business there."

"This isn't the 1950s," Harbaugh answered. "There are ad agencies everywhere. New York is already overpopulated with firms. You wouldn't last a month there."

"But all those small firms you're worried about, they don't have Audi," Jason said. "Put a location in New York and Creative Productions is another big agency that can compete with anyone. And we'd still have clout in the Midwest, as well as the East Coast."

Harbaugh had climbed the corporate ladder by taking chances and pursuing big ideas. He couldn't help himself from thinking about it.

"New York," Harbaugh paused. "How many would you need?"

"We keep it small," Jason said. "Six to ten associates in a small office. We poach a few clients from New York ad agencies and build from there."

"That's going to take a long time," Harbaugh said.

"Six months," Jason said. "Everyone knows the name. We just have to establish ourselves."

"Why didn't you come to me with this before you disappeared?" Harbaugh asked.

"Because I used that time to realize that this is what I want," Jason said. "Remember when I told you that I didn't care about money or recognition? It's because I don't. I want to create something important, something vital, something successful and build the ad firm in a tough city."

"It will be expensive for us," Harbaugh said. "Expansion isn't cheap, especially in New York City."

"Keep everyone on a low base salary," Jason said. "We make it all results-based, that will make everyone work harder. And it will help me prove myself to you again."

"How do I know you won't run away like you just did?" Harbaugh asked.

"Because once you're in New York City, there *is* no place to run," Jason said.

"I'm going to have you sign a contract," Harbaugh said.

"I'm fine with that," Jason said.

Harbaugh reached his hand out to Jason.

"I'm willing to do this," Harbaugh said. "But it's all going to fall on you. You're going to be leading a team in New York City."

Jason shook Harbaugh's hand.

"I can give you six months, that's all I want to budget for, if it isn't working then, I'll be shutting it down," Harbaugh said.

After Harbaugh told Jason they'd meet again to talk

further about the venture, the CEO returned to the elevator to ride to the 27th floor. Jason waited for the elevator to arrive before calling an elevator to go to the 33rd floor.

He hadn't seen Grace in weeks, so he hoped to catch her before she left for lunch. He passed an empty receptionist's desk and headed to Grace's office.

"You're the last person in the world I expected to see walk through the door today," Grace said.

"How've you been?" Jason said, attempting to sound endearing.

"Jason don't start me with a 'how have you been' you just vanished with Brooklyn for a week and I didn't hear a word from either one of you," Grace scolded.

"It was only four days," Jason smiled.

"What's wrong with you?" Grace said.

Jason laughed and shrugged off an answer.

"Are Brooklyn and you playing house now?" Grace asked. "Aaron told me he wouldn't let her stay at their place, so she is staying with you, I assume."

Grace didn't let Jason answer.

"I don't know how much Aaron and her talk, but he's moving back to Cincinnati in a few weeks, so she should probably get the rest of her things."

"Are you disappointed in me?" Jason interrupted.

"I'm not disappointed," Grace shook her head. "It's what I expected of you, no offense. I don't know you very well, but something about you makes me feel you're disconnected from everyone. All this tearing apart you're doing doesn't really bother you."

"What're you trying to say?" Jason asked.

"You act like you connect people to the world, when really, you're disconnecting people from their world," Grace said. "And you don't really care what happens after that. You just want them to be disconnected and broken like you."

Jason plainly looked at her, unable to formulate a response.

"You know I still have to show you something," Grace said.

Jason smiled, "I did agree to it if you helped me with Brooklyn...but you never told me what it was."

"It's going to help you, it's going to change the way you think, even if only for a few days," Grace said.

"I don't mind change, as long as I'm not the one doing it," Jason said.

Grace shook her head, smiled and brushed her hand away as if to say she had seen enough of Jason Vaughn for one day.

With the elevators crowding as people left for lunch, Jason was pushed back into a corner as he rode down from the 33rd floor. His greatest fear arrived as the elevator stopped at the 27th floor: he worried an employee from Creative Productions would notice him.

He slumped down in the back corner to avoid any detection. A lone employee from Creative Productions staggered inside the elevator. Rick Stanberry feebly walked in. Without noticing Jason, Stanberry slowly turned and faced forward as the elevator doors closed.

He looks terrible. That tumor was only a month ago, now he seems like he's moments away from his dying breath.

As the elevator doors opened on the first floor, the crowd encircling Stanberry left the elevator. The frail middle-aged man could sense someone was left in the elevator, but didn't have the strength to turn around to speak to anyone face-to-face. Jason stood in the back corner frightened that the deathly ill version of the man he once hated would turn around.

Stanberry mumbled "Go on ahead, I'll probably slow you down."

For three years, Stanberry had slowed Jason's progress at Creative Productions, limiting his work and doubting his effort. Only now, could Stanberry realize his restraining approach, but at the expense of thinking a stranger was behind him.

Jason stood in the back corner silently until Stanberry left the elevator. As Stanberry crept along in the building's lobby, Jason took a side exit to avoid his former boss.

He found his car and drove back to his apartment. When Jason got out of his car, a forgotten face met him at his front steps.

"You didn't even say goodbye to me," Megan said and slapped Jason across the face.

He looked toward Megan with his face still stinging.

"You lied to me, you cheated on me, you deceived me," Megan yelled. "All of it with one of my good friends, and then you don't have the respect or courtesy to even break up with me."

Megan continued to voice her frustration.

"I don't care about Brooklyn. You're going to screw her

over like you do every other girl in your life, but it's going to be even worse for her since she left her future husband. All you are is destructive. Why would you do this to me?"

She didn't come for an explanation or an answer to any of her questions. She doesn't want to hear an apology or be asked for forgiveness. She just wants to say what she wants to say. Sometimes people need to say what they want to say so they can feel better afterwards.

He could have dismissed her comments and let her leave his life without any understanding of him, but Jason tried to offer some depth into who he believed he was. Megan never had the ability to reach beyond the basics of Jason's life, whether it was because she didn't want to know or couldn't understand, Jason didn't know.

He'd never given her any soluble answer to the man he believed he'd become or why, so for once, he gave her the best thing came to mind.

"I'm not like you and I don't know why," Jason paused. "I don't know who I am because I don't feel what I should feel as a human being, so I have to fake everything. I'm harmful to everyone I'm around because I'm irreparably broken."

Megan was dissatisfied with Jason's response. She turned away and left him standing on the front steps of his apartment. Jason could feel the lingering sting on the side of his face and took a seat on the concrete steps in front of his door.

A single small white daffodil poked out of the black mulch in the flower bed along the side of his apartment. Jason could sense springtime in the air.

34

With the move to New York City approaching, Jason exhausted his energy by writing. He knew once he began building the satellite branch for Creative Productions, he wouldn't have time to write.

He wanted his first novel completed before he left Louisville because he feared it would remain unfinished for years if he didn't. The life of an ad man clawing for business in New York City gave no moments for leisurely writing and literature.

When Brooklyn came back to the apartment after work, she and Jason would browse online through apartments on the Lower East Side or Greenwich Village. Their social circle was collapsing, so neither felt any remorse leaving Louisville.

Brooklyn had told a few of her friends and family about her decision to move away while Jason hadn't found it necessary to tell anyone close to him about his intentions to leave.

Brooklyn's boss, Jerome Felton, had been in pharmaceutical sales for so long he told Brooklyn he could get her a job anywhere in the country. She'd worked for him for three years, so she felt guilty about leaving him, but he comforted her by saying he knew 'this time was coming as soon as she walked through those doors on her first day.'

Harbaugh assured Jason the company would cover hotel expenses for the first two weeks as they established their new living arrangements. Jason texted Harbaugh daily to stay informed on the progression of the venture.

With the thought of moving to New York just a few weeks away, Jason decided accountability was his best choice for his final days in Louisville. He returned to Business Weekly's office Thursday evenings to copy edit and submit the publication for printing.

It had been more than a month since he had last performed his responsibility as copy editor, but he sent out a few emails to explain his disappearance.

As the sun set into the pinkish gold sky, Jason made his way to the office. After a few minutes of driving, he received a phone call from Harbaugh.

"How's everything shaping up?" Jason asked.

"It's looking good Jason, I made a few phone calls and we have the office set up," Harbaugh said. "I'm cutting you back to six people up there. We'll see how that goes first."

"Besides me, who else do you have picked out?" Jason asked.

"Don't worry about that yet," Harbaugh said. "I'll be up there with you the first few weeks."

"I can't believe this is happening so fast," Jason said. "Have you told anyone about it?"

"The necessary people know, but don't go around spreading it," Harbaugh said. "I want us to surprise everyone."

"I don't have anyone to tell anyway," Jason said.

"Good," Harbaugh paused. "One more thing, come in next Friday to the Louisville office. I want to meet with you and everyone else."

"Are you sure they'll let me in the office?" Jason joked.

Harbaugh laughed and said, "I think they'll make an exception this time."

The conversation ended, allowing Jason to envision himself walking around New York City in a suit with Brooklyn by his side.

He went into the Business Weekly's office and noticed everything seemed plainer, duller and more unremarkable. What waited ahead was so vastly better than everything in Louisville that these final weeks were drudgery.

Jason had been in the office for a little more than an hour before Ashley walked in. He realized the next couple Thursdays would be the last few times he'd ever see her.

Someone like Ashley will never make it out of her monotonous and ill-contented life. She's going to live falsely satisfied while my life gets better and better. Her mind is sedated.

"Why Jason Vaughn, I thought you'd be in New York City by now," Ashley smiled.

"No, I have a few weeks left, I thought it'd only be right to finish this out," Jason said.

"We're going to miss you. Well, at least I will," Ashley said.

"I'll be stuck with some new copy editor. What are you going up there for anyway?"

"I'm going to start fresh," Jason said. "I'm going to build the life I want there."

"You're going to need to talk to your doctor, that's going to take some serious memory loss drugs," Ashley joked.

As Jason read through pages, he remembered when he first walked into the Business Weekly's office and offered his services. He thought about how young he'd been, directly out of college looking for some extra money to go along with his entry level advertising position. He thought of how the beginning of his employment at Business Weekly had been the best part of his work week.

Two years later, he couldn't wait to finish the pages and submit the final product for printing. Jason finished his duties, as did Ashley, a little before 10 p.m.

The two walked out together and moved toward their lone cars in the empty parking lot. Before they went into their cars, Ashley asked Jason another question.

"Are you running away or are you searching for something?"

"I just want to know I'm alive," Jason said.

Though it was a cool night, spring was in the air, enough so that Jason rolled down the windows on the ride back to his apartment. He let the cool night air rush through his body as he traveled down city roads. He felt reinvigorated with the changing of seasons.

Everything seemed to be trending upward for him. He had

Brooklyn by his side, he was writing and he had New York City waiting for him in a few weeks.

When he reached his apartment, he paused outside of the window and gazed upon Brooklyn as she worked on her laptop. Jason hadn't discovered the intricacies of her life and didn't yet understand who she was, but he knew that she looked beautiful in her white V-neck. He walked inside.

"I found the perfect apartment," Brooklyn said.

Jason sat beside Brooklyn as she scrolled the screen showing him the apartment that interested her. The small apartment in the Upper East Side would be the Garden of Eden, and Jason and Brooklyn would become the 21st century's Adam and Eve. But in this version, Jason had assured himself no one would pluck an apple from a tree to ruin everything. This time, he knew they could be perfect.

"We won't have to worry about who we were here," Jason said. "Once we move there, no one will know us. We'll be new and unblemished. We can finally be who we want to be."

Brooklyn and Jason chatted for a few minutes in the living room, excited about their new life together, but eventually decided to walk outside to look at the night sky.

As Brooklyn looked up at the stars, Jason wondered how long all of this could last with her. He wondered how long they could stay together. He wondered if New York would enhance their relationship or break everything apart.

Brooklyn and Jason stood together under the stars, unable to understand or decipher who the other person was, because neither of them wanted to know.

35

Jason woke 15 minutes before Brooklyn on the Friday he was scheduled to return to Creative Productions for the meeting set by Harbaugh. He watched her softly breathe as she slept.

Jason picked a white dress shirt and dark checkered tie with his black suit. He drank a glass of orange juice in his dark and quiet apartment. Brooklyn came forth from the bedroom wearing a crème colored dress and a red cardigan.

With the morning darkness waning, the two walked to their cars.

"Do you have to be in at a certain time?" Brooklyn asked.

"Yeah, but I've got a bit of time," Jason said.

"It's still early enough," Brooklyn said. "Do you want to watch the sunrise?"

Jason nodded his head and stepped away from his car. The two walked to a small hill behind the apartment complex. The hill was high enough to see over the buildings and trees that surrounded the apartments, so they were able to see the horizon. Soon, the sun began to make its climb, poking through the darkness and announcing its presence for the day.

The dark night clouds were fueled with light and color, lifting the entire sky.

While the youthful sunrise continued to grow, Brooklyn and Jason stood next to each other silently as the light began to fill their faces. In that moment on the bare hill, there was no other company of life or existence of other beings, it was simply Jason Vaughn, Brooklyn Turner and the rising sun.

The undeniable youth of the two paired with a young sunrise formed together to create incorruptible potential. The moment, the day, the rest of their lives stood before them, and like the sunrise, it would all eventually come, but the beauty of the unknown was the best part, as it always was for Jason.

As the sun moved higher in the sky, the day was upon Jason and Brooklyn. The sunrise had passed, so the two walked down the hill to return to their cars. When they reached the cars, Jason kissed Brooklyn.

"No sunrise is ever the same," Brooklyn said.

Before Jason could think of the right words to say, Brooklyn closed her door and started the engine.

Jason stood in front of his car as he watched Brooklyn drive off toward the sunrise they'd just watched. After a moment of contemplation, Jason made his way to Creative Productions.

Jason straightened his tie before the elevator doors opened on the 27th floor. He remembered how miserable and apathetic this office space had once made him feel, but now, he only had to be engaged for a few hours, planning his move to New York City.

Creative Productions' employees looked twice and stared

as Jason walked toward the conference room. The reappearance of Jason Vaughn surprised everyone except the three men sitting in the conference room.

James Downing, Paul Harbaugh and Rick Stanberry circled around the large table. Jason didn't expected Stanberry to be present in the meeting, but he greeted all three men. Everyone was cordial despite the indisputable fact that Jason had abandoned Creative Productions a month earlier. The conference room fell silent, forcing Jason to ask the first question.

"Is anyone else coming today from the team going to New York," he said.

"No, it's just you today and that's why we wanted to bring you in," Harbaugh said.

Jason acknowledged Harbaugh with a nod, but didn't want to interrupt the silence again. The room was still for a few moments until Harbaugh cut in.

"As you may know by now, Rick isn't doing well," Harbaugh said.

Stanberry nodded.

"With his health issues, he decided to resign from his role as Creative Director," Harbaugh said.

Three years too late. It took a cancerous tumor to get him out of this place.

"When you pitched me the idea about setting up a branch in New York," Harbaugh paused. "I started talking with James about how we wanted to handle the situation. We came to the best possible solution for all of us."

"Jason, you've been so good for us the past few years," Downing said. "It took a little convincing, but we want you to take over as Creative Director here."

"Rick vouched for you so much it was practically my only choice," Harbaugh smiled.

Jason tried to process what was being said. He asked the most essential question in his mind.

"What about New York?" Jason said.

"Don't you get it," Harbaugh said. "You don't have to go to New York. You're taking over as Creative Director. You're not getting your old job back. You're getting a promotion."

The youngest man in the room felt hopeless as his dream disappeared.

"But last week everything was set," Jason said with frustration building. "You told me people were lined up. You said you were going to stay in New York for two weeks."

"I know," Harbaugh answered. "I wanted to see how committed you were to the company and the leadership role you would be willing to take. It showed me you were the right person for this position."

"You lied to me," Jason said. "You told me not to tell anyone about our plan because our plan wasn't even real."

"I did what I had to do to make sure that you were put in the right place," Harbaugh said firmly.

"Why would I ever want to work for someone that pulled all this on me?" Jason shouted.

"Because you don't have a choice," Harbaugh laughed. "You might think that you want to be free, but this is all you know, this is all you can do. And if that wasn't true, you wouldn't have come back here in the first place. So come next Monday, I'm damn sure you'll be sitting at your desk, ready to take over as Creative Director of the Louisville branch."

Harbaugh shook his head, smirking, and walked out of the conference room.

Downing and Stanberry were left with Jason.

"Look Jason, this is a great opportunity for you, No one has come back from what you did and no one this young has ever been offered this position," Downing said.

"It was all lies," Jason meekly responded.

"You have another week off, come in next Monday and Rick will show you everything," Downing said. "You've worked with everyone you will be directing."

"I'll be here for two weeks to help you transition into the new position," Stanberry said. "Everything will be easy."

"And what am I going to say when people ask where I've been for the past month?" Jason asked.

"We already told everyone you went on a two-week vacation followed by a training program for the management position you're about to lead," Downing said.

Jason shook his head in disgust.

"Why can't anyone be honest?" Jason said.

"In this situation, the truth is more damaging," Downing said. "You're out of a job if the truth matters that much."

Downing excused himself from the conference room, leaving the two former rivals sitting across from each other.

"I'm glad it's you taking my position," Stanberry looked at Jason. "You're the only person I wanted to take over for me."

Jason ran his hand through his hair and slouched in his chair, signifying defeat. Stanberry feebly rose and patted Jason on the shoulder.

"I'll see you next Monday," Stanberry said.

With his dream gone and the chance of escape ruined, Jason walked toward the elevator. He could feel his heart plummeting on the somber ride to the lobby. He walked to the nearest restaurant and sat at an empty bar before the lunch crowd filled the place. He asked the bartender for a whiskey sour.

By noon, Jason had spent all his cash.

By one, he was ineptly intoxicated. He left the restaurant and walked to the Waterfront Park. He watched the Ohio River pass by and moved along the concrete paths shaded by the blossoming trees.

Jason realized the lying and narcissism had to stop. He had lived the wrong way for too long, guided by selfishness. As Harbaugh had deceived him, Jason had fooled and cheated so many victims prior to today. He was disgusted by himself.

He sat on a park bench watching the river as grey clouds filled the sky. Raindrops started to fall, but Jason stayed on the bench. As the rain fell harder, Jason looked toward the sky, allowing rain drops to splash on his face. He raised his arms asking, "What else will there be, is this all life will be?"

The rainy afternoon passed. Jason was sober enough to drive to his apartment. When he returned to his apartment, he noticed the lone white daffodil in the flower bed had been destroyed by the hard rain fall.

Before he stepped inside his apartment, he took off his drenched suit jacket and water-logged shoes.

He unlocked the door and placed his suit jacket on the kitchen counter.

As he walked further inside and turned on a light, he saw the shine of a silver key resting on the countertop.

Jason closed his eyes and took a deep breath. With his eyes still closed he exhaled. Then Jason reopened his eyes, ready to face the world that had dramatically changed since the sunrise. He walked into his bedroom to confirm his assumption. Brooklyn's clothes were gone. There was no makeup or toiletries in the bathroom.

There was no sign of Brooklyn Turner's existence, merely a shiny silver key resting on the countertop.

36

*B*rooklyn had disappeared from Jason's life, and he had yet to try to find her a week later. He hadn't called her once or sent a text. Brooklyn had promptly faded from Jason's life and he saw no reason to chase an already vanished illusion.

It didn't matter where she went, who she was with or what she'd do, Jason knew Brooklyn was gone and she wouldn't reappear. And even if he were to see her again, Jason planned to nod his head and smile with complete brevity that their moment of perfection had long since passed, washed over by the cleansing ocean waves and burned away by the rising sun.

No moment had ever been too great for Jason, but he enjoyed thinking of the subtle precursor of everything before Brooklyn and how their fleeting moment together had started.

Jason would never wish back the time he spent watching the sunrise or staring at the night skies with Brooklyn. But if there was ever a single moment Jason could have back, he wanted it to be second before he saw her for the first time.

The unknown and unmarked potential of the future had always been the best part for Jason, and it always would be.

When he looked at Brooklyn for the first time, the limitless and untapped possibilities were before him, the undefined future was preeminent. Even if he were to chase Brooklyn, the moment he so desperately desired had already passed because in that moment of indefinite potential, there was no thought of the pursuit of Brooklyn Turner, no thought of what would happen while they were together or the impending ending. The only thought in that moment was what could be, the potential of what might happen was better than finding out what would happen.

As Jason sat in his apartment finishing his novel during his final week of unemployment, he didn't think once of a way to bring Brooklyn back. Their moment together had slowly risen like a sunrise, and then moved high into the sky, but eventually, it faded away in the sunset. A new day had come, so Jason's only choice was to continue to move forward knowing he had already seen the best sunrise.

By Friday afternoon, Jason put the final touches on his novel. He spent Friday evening skimming through his work with no urge to pursue any social opportunities.

After being isolated in his apartment for an entire week, Jason gave into his friends' request on Saturday night to socialize. Like he had done so many nights before, Jason went to Circle's to meet the usual group for the typical night out.

It was the first time in almost ten months that Jason had gone out with his friends without a girl by his side. They knew better than to ask him about Brooklyn and his plans to pursue her.

With rumors spreading about Jason's reappearance at

Creative Productions, they were comfortable questioning his career. Julie asked if he was returning to his old job.

"I'm supposed to be there Monday morning at nine, but I don't want to go back," Jason told his friends circled around him. "I can't. I don't want to live in that boredom again."

Julie tried to convince Jason that he couldn't pass on the opportunity, but after a few minutes of debate, Keshawn pulled Jason aside to walk around the bar.

The two moved around the bar talking to the people they saw there often. The two usually avoided asking about each other's personal life, but Jason had an odd impulse to hear about Keshawn's.

"You're still with Heather, right?" Jason asked.

"Yep, almost a year now," Keshawn said.

"Have you ever lied to her?" Jason said.

"No, I haven't," Keshawn said. "I guess I haven't ever had the need to."

Jason nodded his head as the two continued to walk around the bar. They found Julie, Kyle and Naomi in a corner and joined their conversation.

A little past 1 a.m., Circle reached its full capacity. Jason shuffled through the crowd and socialized with familiar faces while feeling youth exuded from the wooden floors and loud music. He stood at the bar waiting for another drink and Heather joined him.

"Looking for Brooklyn?" she asked.

"No." Jason smiled sadly.

The bartender handed Jason his drink, he grinned and

tipped his glass to Heather before walking away. It was nearly 3 a.m. when the group of friends decided to leave. Keshawn and Heather walked down the street to an Uber. As the couple climbed into the car, Keshawn called to Jason, who stood across the street.

"Jason, let's get lunch together Monday," he said.

Jason nodded and waved in agreement.

This'll be the last time I see him. By the time he's sitting at his desk Monday morning, I'm going to be anywhere but Louisville.

After spending a final night with his friends, Jason decided he needed a new start. He planned to drive into the sunrise, just as Brooklyn had done, never to be seen again. He didn't know where he would go or what he'd do, but he knew escaping from his previous life to restart a new one was his only choice.

Kyle guided Julie to his car as Naomi and Jason followed a few steps behind.

"See you later," Julie waved.

A few steps later, Jason and Naomi reached their separate cars. Before Naomi opened her car door, Jason looked at her.

"If anyone knows, it's you," Jason paused. "Why can't I be good?"

Naomi shook her head, sensing the desperation in Jason's voice.

"Jason, you say you want to be a good, but deep down, that isn't who you are," Naomi said. "You might think you want to change, but you really don't."

"Well, where should I go from here?" he said.

"Stop hiding from who you are, don't deny it," Naomi

said. "It only prevents you from truly changing into a better person."

Jason said goodnight to her.

"I don't know if I'll be seeing you again," Jason said. "Take care of yourself; make sure everyone stays in line."

"I know you well enough to know that I'll be seeing you soon," Naomi said.

"No, this time is different," Jason assured her. "I need to be free."

Naomi ran her hand through her hair.

"We want to be free, but if the cage we're trapped in was unlocked, we still wouldn't leave it," Naomi said.

Jason shook his head, before Naomi continued.

"But do you want to know a secret?" Naomi asked. "It's always been unlocked for us."

Naomi smiled and walked to her car.

Jason watched her drive off before getting into his car to return to his apartment. On the ride back, he recalled the events and conversations of the night. He wondered if it was the last time he'd see all of them together. He wondered if he could disappear like Brooklyn.

He left his friends behind on his note. Keshawn and he planning a lunch that would never come, Julie drunkenly waving goodbye and Naomi filling him with a final piece of self-actualization.

37

When he returned to his apartment, the night faded away as he slowly fell asleep, but not before he caught a glimpse of the night sky. As he looked at the stars, he wondered if Brooklyn Turner was looking at the same vastness of sky.

On Monday morning, Stanberry walked into his office at the usual time of 8:45 a.m. On his way in, Stanberry glanced at the desk that should be occupied by Jason Vaughn, but saw no sign of the young man that was set to replace him.

It was a few minutes past 9 a.m. when Stanberry closed his door and returned to his desk to sit down. Several minutes later, Stanberry heard a soft knock on his door and it slowly opened.

"Jason, where have you been?"

"Sorry I'm late, I was caught in traffic," Jason said.

"Go ahead and get settled in," Stanberry said. "We're meeting with the team in an hour to reintroduce you to everyone."

Downing, Stanberry, Jason and the creative team gathered in the 27th floor conference room just after 10 a.m.

After Stanberry went through a few updates, Downing took charge of the room.

"Mr. Stanberry's health has become a concern for everyone," Downing said. "He's given so much to this company and we owe him even more in return, but he's decided it's time to step down."

Downing told the associates how Stanberry, Harbaugh and he had decided Jason would be the best person to fill the vacancy, and to reward Jason for his diligent effort, they rewarded him with a sudden vacation before the promotion. Downing described how they believed Jason needed management and leadership training for the position, so his extended absence was due to the training program.

With the associates believing every word Downing said, he introduced Jason as the new Creative Director.

"Thank you, I'm glad to be back," Jason said to everyone in the room. "It seems like I've been gone a while, but the time helped me prepare for the position."

Live in the lie.

"The management and leadership training course I took helped me understand what I need to do for us to be successful as possible. The most important thing I learned is to value communication."

Jason looked at Stanberry and Downing.

Live in the lie.

"Mr. Stanberry was a tremendous leader for us all these years, and I'll do my best to be the same," Jason continued.

"He was by our side and a leader who was always honest with us. I guarantee that you can expect the same from me."

Live in the lie.

The associates softly clapped for Jason without doubting any of his capabilities.

Stanberry explained how the transition would only take two weeks, leaving everyone satisfied that Jason would know the intricacies of the position.

The associates emptied the conference room and left Jason with Downing and Stanberry.

"I'm glad you decided to come back to us, now it's time to get to work," Downing said. He nodded his head and left the room to return to the 28th floor.

Stanberry shrugged his shoulders and weakly walked out of the room.

Alone in the conference room, Jason looked out through the glass windows to the city below. He watched cars and people moved around the street, hustling to their next moment in life.

There was nothing for him to say. No one would listen.

He turned and looked around the 27th floor of Creative Productions.

With the thought of a fading smile, thinning hair and middle age creeping closer toward him, Jason walked back to his desk, his lost youth behind him and the unbearable boredom of his future lying ahead.

Dedication

To Alexis Draut for her excellent editing suggestions.

.